# TWELVE DAYS OF FAERY

### SHARDS OF A BROKEN SWORD: BOOK ONE

## W.R. GINGELL

Cover by MerryBookRound

Twelve Days of Faery and the Shards of a Broken Sword Trilogy are copyright © 2019 by W.R. Gingell

All rights reserved.

No part of this book may be reproduced in any form or by any electronic or mechanical means, including information storage and retrieval systems, without written permission from the author, except for the use of brief quotations in a book review.

❦ Created with Vellum

*Many thanks to Jack Heckel,
whose delightful work gave me
the story-seed that became
TWELVE DAYS OF FAERY.*

# 1

## DAY ONE

There's a fine line between the perception of coincidence and intent when it comes to a series of unfortunate events. Three dead fiancées, two lost sweethearts, and a few mutilated flirts tended to slip from the realms of coincidence and into that of deliberate misadventure, thought King Markon. The fiancées, sweethearts and flirts were not his: they belonged—or *had* belonged—to his son, Prince Parrin.

King Markon sighed. It had been easy to dismiss the first fiancée as dreadful happenstance. The child had fallen from her horse, after all. And the second, a younger princess from the neighbouring kingdom, had been attacked by bandits in her own lands.

At first the danger had only been to fiancées. Then, as Markon grew wise to the problem and discouraged immediate thoughts of marriage, Parrin's sweethearts began to have unfortunate accidents as well. Parrin fell in love so quickly, even for a boy of twenty, that it was hard to keep the girls out of danger. It wasn't until Parrin's first sweetheart vanished without a trace that the murmurs began. To Markon's astonishment, the murmurs only doubled the interest in his son. It was spoken in whispers around the kingdom that any woman who freed the prince from his curse, be she shepherdess or princess, would marry the prince and be queen in the course of time.

The first three girls could be blamed on the curse, if curse there was. The others, thought Markon, with a surge of sudden distaste for himself, could only be laid at his own door. He'd heard the rumours; and instead of squashing them, he'd allowed them to run their course, hoping that one of the girls *would* be able to break the curse. There hadn't been any shortage of them, and he'd personally vetted the few determined young women who pretended to be Parrin's fiancées after the real ones died. Each of those young ladies had died, disappeared, or been injured grievously within a week of being affianced to Parrin.

King Markon pulled distractedly at the silvering hair at his temples. There was a lot more of it there lately, along with a suspicious thinning of hair at the top of his head. Stress, Parrin told him. Markon was more inclined to think that he was simply getting old. Still, the stress didn't help; and now his steward had come to him with the unwelcome news that an enchantress had come to try her luck at the curse.

On one hand, thought Markon, struggling to decide if he should allow the enchantress to do her best or if he should send her safely on her way; an enchantress really ought to be able to take care of herself. On the other, the curse's latest victim was a poor noble maiden who had merely chanced to catch Parrin's eye and exchange a flirtatious smile with him. Markon wasn't sure the unfortunate girl's hair would ever regrow. That was the sort of thing a woman took seriously, enchantress or not.

The steward, who had been waiting with commendable patience while his master thought the matter through, ventured to say politely: "Sire, should I bid the enchantress enter?"

"Why not?" said Markon tiredly. The only other option was to lock Parrin in his suite where unwary damsels wouldn't catch his eye. "Send her in."

He was gazing out the window when the steward announced: "Althea of Avernse, your majesty."

Markon turned his head to meet a dark blue pair of eyes that were quiet, shuttered, and surprisingly sharp. The owner of those eyes curtseyed in a short, precise manner, her gaze never leaving him, and then folded her hands in front of her. She was less...enchantressy...than Markon expected. Part of that, he was ruefully aware, was because he was getting rather old, and Althea looked ridiculously young. The other part of it was the sensible, well-cut frock of blue cotton that had not a glitter of the kind of decorative magical furbelows that enchantresses usually sported. Her back was as straight as a poker, prim and no-nonsense, and her hair was braided to within an inch of its life without so much as daring to curl at her temples, though it was plainly aching to do so. Markon thought of the little countess sprawled in the courtyard at her horse's feet, the weaver's daughter and her horror at her severed hand, and the two lost ladies.

He said instinctively: "I'm sorry, but we're no longer accepting applications."

Her head jerked back, surprise and—was that annoyance?—on her face. It was gone almost immediately: Althea's eyes narrowed on him in distinct interest. "Is that so? I was under the impression that the curse was still very much in effect."

"It is."

"I see." Althea let the words hang in the air, turning over her own thoughts; and Markon, who should have called back the steward and had him show the child out, simply watched her think. She was too old for Parrin, of course, by a good five years or so.

*And far too young for you*, thought Markon, startling himself with the direction his thoughts had taken him. Besides, an older woman might be just the thing for the boy.

"I'm curious," said Althea. While he had been thinking, she had come to her own conclusions, and was now watching him.

"Why not just have another child?" Her eyes swept over him, absorbed and assessing, and Markon felt a slight warmth creeping up his neck to the back of his ears. "You're young enough to marry again. Handsome, too: you wouldn't have any problem finding a wife."

She took a lot upon herself, this enchantress! thought Markon. But that was enchantresses for you: they considered themselves equal with royalty– at the very least. He said, with gentle sarcasm: "Being king helps with that, too."

Althea's eyes grew deeper blue: a sign of amusement, Markon thought. "So you did think of it."

"Of course. An heir who can't fall in love and marry can't produce an heir of his or her own."

"You thought the same thing would happen to any other child you sired," she said accurately.

"Yes. We don't know who cursed Parrin, or what the curse entails– we don't even know that it *is* a curse."

"What will you do, then?"

Markon caught himself tugging at his silver hairs again and folded his arms instead. "Lock Parrin up. Choose another line of succession. Find someone to investigate the curse from the outside. As a matter of fact, Wyndsor–"

"I can investigate from the outside," said Althea, as Markon's inevitable reflections on the subject of Wyndsor caused his sentence to trail away. "I think it makes more sense to investigate from the inside, but we couldn't depend on his highness to fall in love with me, after all. And if it makes you uncomfortable–"

"It's not about my comfort," said Markon, unsure whether he was exasperated at Althea or at the thought that it would be only too easy for Parrin to fall in love with her. "Perhaps I should take you to the infirmary. You might like to see the young ladies who have been unfortunate enough to fall foul of the curse."

Althea gazed at him in silence for a few moments. Then she

smiled; a brilliant, joyous smile that transformed her serious face and took his breath away. "That would be very useful," she said.

*Useful!* thought Markon, as he strolled the Long Gallery with Althea on his arm. Stroll was perhaps a weak word for what they were doing: Althea stepped purposefully, entirely without the sedate glide that usually characterised the walk of an enchantress. She actually seemed to *bounce*, her interest palpable. Why would she find a viewing of the young ladies afflicted by the curse to be useful?

She wouldn't, Markon realised, unless she was already investigating the curse. He sent a keen look down at her, amused and slightly irritated, and when Althea glanced up to meet his gaze he thought he saw a delicate flush of colour come and go on the cheek closest to him.

"These young ladies in the infirmary," she said, rather hurriedly. "Why keep them here? I assume they *have* families."

"They do."

"You feel responsible."

"I *am* responsible."

"I expect you paid their families, too," said Althea thoughtfully, with another look up at him.

"Through here," Markon said, avoiding the question. The cheek of the child! She was laughing at him! He thought he saw approval in her blue eyes along with the amusement, and felt a little better. "Some of them are rather badly hurt. Try not to disturb them more than you must."

That took the amusement out of her eyes. She nodded, and followed him into the infirmary.

The infirmary wasn't exactly an infirmary, as such. Like the gallery that adjoined it, it was a vast room that ran along the outside wall of the west wing: but where the Long Gallery had a massive tapestry or oil painting every couple of hundred yards, the infirmary had been divided into smaller suites. Eight of the ten suites were occupied by various of Parrin's young ladies and a few of the enterprising women who had sought to break the curse. Markon approached the fourth of these and knocked politely on the door. He could have taken Althea to the first room, which contained only the young lady with the lost hair, but he felt that he would like to discourage her as strongly as possible.

The door was opened by a tall, neat nurse with a capable face and even more capable hands. She curtseyed deeply to Markon, and nearly as deeply to Althea, who looked her swiftly up and down, and said: "You studied at Holbrooks, didn't you?"

The nurse went very slightly pink. "I did, lady. How did you know?"

"I'd know that technique anywhere," said Althea, rather to Markon's bemusement. She was looking at the nurse's hands, but he had the distinct impression that she was seeing a lot more than he did. "You're very talented."

"Thank you, lady. Will you come in?"

There was a furrow between Althea's brows, straight and deep. Once again, Markon wasn't sure what it was she was seeing, but it was evident that it surprised her. She advanced on the bed carefully, and he would have thought she was suffering from a weak stomach if it wasn't for the fact that her eyes frequently darted to things he couldn't see. It looked as though she was studying a vast, complicated whole instead of one broken young girl. At last she said: "That's a bit of a mess, isn't it?"

"I've never seen anything like it," said the nurse. "Every bone in her body was broken: shattered to pieces. And as soon as I get one of them fixed and go onto the next, the spell creeps back and undoes all my work."

"Is she always unconscious?"

"It seemed kinder," said Markon, avoiding the sight of the girl's bruised and swollen body by keeping his eyes solely on Althea.

She laid one hand on the girl's rubber-like arm and asked: "Did she fall from some height?"

"A foot-high dais."

"I see." Althea didn't look surprised. "It's a nasty bit of magic: a spell I haven't seen before. I believe that if we could heal her fast enough to beat the re-shattering, having her whole body reknit all at once would break the loop."

"I thought so, too," said the nurse. "But I couldn't equal the rate of shattering *or* heal enough bones at once."

"If I slowed the rate of shattering, do you think you could heal her completely?"

Markon frowned. "I thought the magic was unfamiliar to you."

"Not the magic: the spell. I know the *type* of magic very well."

"I thought I knew every variant of magic that there is," said the nurse. "What is it?"

"It's not something you would have come across," said Althea. "I'll come back tomorrow to help."

"I told you," said Markon. "We're not accepting applications."

"I know," she said, and then to the nurse: "I'll come back tomorrow. We'll need a few hours at least."

Althea left the suite in an energetic bounce. At first, Markon thought she was merely eager to see the other girls, but as they moved swiftly from suite to suite he saw the storminess in those deep blue eyes. She was *angry*. When they were back in the gallery proper, she stood for a full minute in silence with her eyes on the carpeted floor while Markon watched, smiling faintly.

Just as he was beginning to think she wouldn't speak again, Althea said: "This is not acceptable." Her mouth was pursed, her nostrils flaring. "It's ridiculous to allow this to continue: those poor little girls!"

"We're no longer accepting applications," repeated Markon flatly. That eager sense of justice needed to be protected from itself. It was a wonder that Althea, young as she was, hadn't yet dug herself in over her head with some valiant cause or other.

"So you said. But what about those girls? And what happens *next* time something goes wrong?"

"My dear child, you're barely older than my son! How could I live with myself if the curse caught you too?"

Althea gazed at him for a very long time, her mind almost visibly clicking and whirring. She was trying to decide whether or not to tell him something, Markon realised. At last, she said: "Will it help if I tell you that a curse will have absolutely no effect upon me?"

"Yes," said Markon, after a brief, exasperated moment. "Why didn't you tell me immediately?"

"I like to see how things fit together in order," said Althea. "It's a very interesting curse. And there was always the possibility that you–"

She caught herself, looking slightly annoyed, and Markon found that he knew exactly what she had been going to say. "You thought it was possible that it wasn't actually a curse, and that I was responsible for the accidents."

"You wouldn't have been the first homicidal monarch I've met," said Althea apologetically.

Markon tried and failed to suppress a grin. "Are you immune to curses as a whole, or just this one in particular?"

"As a whole," said Althea. She displayed one hand, fingers splayed, and on her index finger Markon saw a vague shadow that could have been a ring if a person squinted at it in the right light. "I have a handy little bauble that blocks that sort of nastiness."

"Do you show it to everyone?" He couldn't help feeling that as a safety measure, a curse-repelling ring everyone knew about wouldn't be particularly effective.

Again, Althea's head jerked up slightly: Markon thought she was surprised.

"No," she said. "But you have nice lines by your eyes. You won't tell anyone."

"Those came with the silver hairs," said Markon regretfully. "You've seen the girls, lady. Ring or no, are you sure you want to attempt this?"

"I'm sure," said Althea. "I've my own demands, of course."

"Of course," echoed Markon. He hadn't doubted it for a moment. The question was, could he afford what she wanted? Enchantresses had a tendency to be expensive.

"I don't want half your kingdom or anything like that," said Althea. "I will need to live in the castle for the duration, of course; and there's the small matter of being made queen at some point. I understand that marriage is still part of the reward?"

"It is," agreed Markon. He would have felt disappointed, but he was almost certain that if he waited long enough, Althea's real motives would slowly but surely surface. What exactly did she want? He didn't think it was Parrin.

However, all Althea said was: "All right. I'll draw up the contract myself. May I see the prince now?"

Markon stiffened. "Of course," he said. He shouldn't be surprised: Parrin was not only a very good catch, he was a very handsome one. Of course Althea meant to marry the boy. "He'll be very glad to meet you."

Still, when he introduced Althea to Parrin, she didn't seem particularly coy. She curtsied to him with less depth than she had curtseyed to Markon, and said in an offhand manner: "You're rather prettier than I expected from the portraits."

Parrin bowed and smiled, but he looked as though he was no more sure than Markon was that he'd been given a compliment.

"I understand that you have a rather difficult problem," continued Althea. She was remarkably business-like for a girl who had just been discussing marriage. Not a maidenly smoothing of the hair or sparkle of the eye. "I have a little bit of an idea about it. May I ask questions?"

"Of course," said Parrin. He was cautiously admiring her, though Markon was pleased to see that he didn't go so far as to smile. The boy was thoughtless, but Markon would like to think that he wasn't so careless as to potentially endanger Althea.

"The first two girls, the fiancées–"

"Yes, lady?"

"Both of those were accounted to be accidents, weren't they?"

"Yes, lady. The countess was thrown from her horse in the courtyard and the princess was attacked by bandits when she returned home from a visit."

"How long between the betrothal and the death for the countess?"

"A few weeks," said Parrin, tugging at the cuffs of his jacket. He had been very fond of the girl, thought Markon with a pang: he had also been the one to find her.

"The princess?"

"A few months."

Althea frowned, a quick, reflexive action. "You weren't immediately engaged again afterward, were you?"

"No: I met Jeannie at court and we stepped out a few times. She disappeared before it even got about that we were thinking of each other. After that it seemed to take less and less to activate the curse."

"What set it off most recently?"

"I smiled at a girl in one of the corridors," said Parrin glumly. Markon couldn't blame him: he remembered what it was like to be Parrin's age, and the idea of being unable to so much as kiss a girl without something unfortunate happening to her was horrible to contemplate.

"And how long was it before it took effect?"

"A few days," said Parrin.

"I see," said Althea. "Don't move, please. You're going to have to hold perfectly still." Parrin nodded, looking rather nonplussed. To Markon she said: "Would you hold this? Thank you," and pressed something circular and metallic into his hand. He looked down at the ring, somehow more real in his hand than it had looked on her finger, and took far too long to realise what she was doing. When he finally did understand, Markon started forward, his hand closing around the ring convulsively. By then Althea was on tiptoes with her hands cupping Parrin's face, kissing the boy with some force and not a little skill if his reaction was anything to judge by.

Markon felt a rush of molten anger unlike anything he'd ever felt before. He didn't think he moved or even thought, caught up in the stunning heat of it, but that was his hand gripping Althea's arm with white fingers and tearing her away from Parrin, and that was his other hand shoving the ring back on her finger, his own slightly shaking.

Althea, her eyes rather big but not at all frightened, said a thoughtful: "Ow," up at him.

It was left to Parrin's rather frantic: "Dad! Dad, she didn't mean any harm!" to bring him to the realisation that he'd clutched Althea to his chest, and that he'd not been gentle about it. Parrin was evidently of the persuasion that his father objected to what could technically be called an assault on a royal personage. Markon, breathing heavily through his nose, released Althea. She hadn't struggled at all and now merely smoothed her dress and hair as though she hadn't just put herself wantonly in danger.

"You said you were going to work from the outside!" Markon said furiously.

"No, I didn't," said Althea, and there was a suggestion of stubbornness to her mouth. "I said I *could* if me working from the inside made you uncomfortable. I also said it would make more sense to investigate from the inside. You didn't object."

"I object!" said Markon in exasperation. "I object *very much!*"

"Well, it's too late now," Althea said reasonably. "And it's proved remarkably useful, too. For instance, I'm now quite sure that you're not dealing with a curse– well, not in any technical sense of the word, anyway."

"What?" demanded Markon, in less than cordial tones.

"I was already pretty certain it wasn't," she told him. "None of the girls have anything clinging to them—well, apart from some rather nasty magic that isn't attached the prince—and neither does the prince. As a matter of fact, they all seem to have– at any rate, I could only be certain that there was no curse by taking off the ring."

"And putting yourself in exactly the kind of danger I didn't want you to be in!" said Markon. "I've a good mind to send you packing!"

"No, you don't," said Althea.

"Of course I don't!" groaned Markon. She'd achieved more in a couple of hours than any of the girls (or in fact any of the enchanters he'd called in) had achieved in the last couple of years.

"Parrin can't be expected to live his life locked away from women–"

"I should think not!" said Parrin feelingly.

"–and it's not good for your kingdom, either. After a while you get people making snide remarks about the crown sacrificing the people on the altar of succession, and then–"

"Small disturbances that become bigger ones," finished Markon, meeting her eyes. "Factions forming across the court and perhaps an accident or two for myself and Parrin."

Althea nodded. "Exactly. I'm rather good at this sort of thing, actually. Try to trust me a little."

"You have a fortnight," said Markon.

## 2

## DAY TWO

*A*lthea brought the contract to him the next day. Markon, who had been restlessly moving about his library all morning in the resolute determination that he was *not* waiting for her, tried to tell his steward that he would be available in a few hours but instead found himself ordering the man to send her straight in.

When she came in, Althea looked decidedly weary. Her hair was braided more tightly than ever, and today she wore a severe black dress that did nothing to soften the fact that she had dark bruises below her eyes and that her skin was decidedly pale.

"Good heavens, what happened?" Markon demanded, surprised into taking a step toward her.

"I don't sleep very well on my first night in a new bed," said Althea, her eyes slipping past him.

Hm. So she was lying to him. No, not lying: withholding. Markon thought about it and came to the conclusion that he knew exactly what she'd been up to before she came to see him. "How did your experiment go?" he asked.

He was rewarded by that brilliant, sudden smile. "*Very* well," she said. "Miss Augusta will make a full recovery, though she'll be bed-bound for a few days yet until her mind recognises that her bones are healed. Mind doesn't take to healing magic as well as bones and flesh do."

Markon, forgetting the contract for the moment, asked: "Is there anything you can do for the others?"

"Nothing that Charlotte isn't already doing," said Althea briskly. She dug briefly through a small satchel and brought out a neatly folded piece of paper, which she passed to Markon. "Though if the sleeping girl–"

"–Rosemary," said Markon, recognising his cue. He unfolded the paper and found a neat, precise, and orderly set of terms. A neat, precise, and orderly signature sat demurely below them.

"Thank you. If Rosemary had a sweetheart before her head was turned by Prince Parrin, it might be a good idea to send him up to kiss her."

Markon ran a jaded eye over the contract and found it to be delightfully straightforward. "Really?"

"Oh yes. They love that sort of thing. They think it's romantic."

"They?" he asked vaguely, signing his own name beside hers. It didn't occur to him until he'd done so that Althea had been watching him very closely. That made him pay attention properly. "What do you mean, *they*?"

"The fae," she said. "They like to play games. They like little puppet people and little puppet romances."

"This was an attack by Faery?"

"I'm not exactly sure yet," said Althea. Her voice sounded troubled. "It's all fae magic, but I'd swear it's from different fae each girl. Some of it is horribly powerful, like Miss Augusta and the first two fiancées, and some of it is more spiteful than anything."

"The girl with the missing hair," nodded Markon. He folded his arms and leaned into his desk.

"You had me sign that contract before you told me about the fae."

Althea flicked her eyes up at him. "I thought you wanted to sign the contract."

"I *did* want to sign–" Markon stopped, and ran his fingers through his hair. "What's your plan?"

"I'll gather a little information, and then I'll try to find the Door that was used."

"A *door*? What door?"

"A Door through to Faery," said Althea. "There are a few things I want to know first, though; and if I'm fortunate I won't need to go through at all."

"There aren't any Doors to Faery here in the castle," objected Markon. "We've got wards and such things on every wall and tower."

"I don't mean a Door from *their* side," Althea said. "I'm looking for a Door from *our* side."

"Who would be stupid enough—not mentioning the small matter of it being treason—to open Doors into Faery?"

"Well, why pick on Prince Parrin?" said Althea reasonably. "For that matter, why magic away a girl's hair? There's a lot I don't know, but what I do know right now is that your subjects have been attacked by several fae. Your wards would prevent Doors being opened from the other side; therefore, someone from this side must be opening them."

"Can you can find one?"

"I think so," said Althea. "I told you: I'm rather good at this. What I'm more interested in knowing is *who* did it."

Markon said bluntly: "I'm more interested in stopping the accidents than knowing who's opening Doors to Faery."

"That's because you haven't thought it through properly," said Althea, standing very straight and still. She was frowning, so deep in thought that Markon knew it didn't occur to her that she'd just insulted him. "If we know who's doing it, we can stop it from this side. It's always a good idea to avoid going into Faery if you possibly can."

"I take it you've spent a great deal of time in Faery," said Markon, with just a feather edge of amusement to his tone. The air of ancient knowledge sat whimsically on her youthful face.

"Oh yes," she said. "I was a changeling."

She couldn't have knocked the smile from his face more thoroughly if she'd said she was troll-stock. "Excuse me?" he said.

That made Althea look up in surprise. She said hastily: "I was stolen, I mean. I'm a human changeling, not fae. I had to claw and trick my way back here every step of the way."

"And the fae?"

Althea went rather blank and stiff. "She'd drowned my little sister in the pond behind my mother's house a few days earlier. She was waterfae, you see. They do that quite a lot: even the little ones. I got rid of her but she had my face and my voice as a glamour and I don't think my mother understood."

"I see," said Markon, feeling sick. "What are the chances that you'll have to go back into Faery for this?"

"Middling to high," said Althea, her voice still carefully blank. "If the Door-opener has been careless about where they open Doors it shouldn't be too hard to find out who did it. If they've been careful I'll have to go straight to Faery and ask questions there."

She gave him a short, regal nod and turned briskly. She was halfway to the door before Markon realised in some bemusement that she had excused herself and was in fact leaving without his dismissal. Before he could stop himself, Markon darted forward and caught her by the wrist. Althea turned on her toes and looked enquiringly at him. "I want daily reports," he said, releasing her wrist with a faint warmth to his cheeks. "More, if you discover anything of importance."

"All right," said Althea. "Will you be available?"

"I'm always available for this particular situation."

Althea's back was as stiff as ever, and her face as serious as before, but he thought she was pleased at his reply.

"One more thing," said Markon. "If it comes to going into Faery, I'm coming with you."

Althea opened her mouth, paused, and seemed to reconsider. "All right," she said. "But we'll have to go at night, when you won't be missed. The last thing we need is a panic because your staff think you've gone missing too."

"Oh, have you misplaced the odd monarch or two?"

"Not exactly," said Althea. To his great amusement she gave him another regal little nod and then swept from the room without answering further.

Markon found himself disagreeably busy after that. The neighbouring kingdom of Wyndsor had kindly (or was it cleverly? he wondered) sent their most respected practitioner of magic, accompanied by an excessively large-nostriled emissary who used those unusually large nostrils to look down on everything he could conceivably look down on. The practitioner of magic had been housed with him in the guest wing of the castle for the past three weeks without any more sign of solving Parrin's problem than the girl with missing hair had shown of the hair growing back. This fact didn't prevent both Doctor and Emissary from eating the best Montalier had to offer, making a nuisance of themselves around the castle generally, *or* popping up in inconvenient and highly suspect places.

Unfortunately, it also didn't prevent Doctor Romalier from bursting into Markon's library a bare half hour after Althea had left it, quivering with indignation from the curled up toes of his pointy shoes to the curled up point of his tiny white beard. Markon looked up at the rattle of the doorknob, his attention snatched away from contemplation of several proposed export and trade contracts.

"Your majesty!" uttered Doctor Romalier.

"I'm beginning to wonder," said Markon, somewhat coldly. He

was prepared to allow Althea to be less than formal because he liked her. He was not prepared to extend the same liberty to the doctor, who already seemed to be taking enough liberties of his own. "Did you lose your way, doctor, and find yourself in my private library through some mistake?"

Doctor Romalier had the presence of mind to bow at once, apologising stiffly and formally, and somehow managed not to say exactly how he'd managed to bypass Markon's steward— or the guard on the only set of stairs that led to the library. Markon as stiffly accepted the apology, regretfully aware from the gleam of righteous indignation in the doctor's eye that the interview was far from over. He would have liked to call his steward and throw the man out, but Wyndsor/Montalier relations were already strained enough without the sort of scandal that would bring.

Instead, he said: "You seem disturbed, Doctor."

Doctor Romalier immediately swelled. "I have just learned, your majesty, that you have engaged a female magic user to break the curse on Prince Parrin!"

"I have," said Markon.

"*Well*, your majesty!"

Markon let his eyes fall conspicuously to the trade agreements in his hand and flicked them back up at the doctor. "You seem disturbed, Romalier. Are your concerns for the fact that I hired another practitioner, or that she's female?"

"I'm certainly not threatened by the investigations of an *enchantress*," said Doctor Romalier stiffly. "If your majesty chooses to hire a woman to do the work of a doctor, that is of course your right. I was merely concerned about the young woman's safety. She is young and fragile."

"She's certainly very young," agreed Markon. "I think you'll find that she's reasonably resilient, however."

"I see," said the doctor coldly. "I'm sorry your majesty felt such a lack of confidence in my abilities, and in Wyndsor's willingness to assist."

"I've never doubted Wyndsor's willingness," said Markon. "However, in Montalier we have a saying, doctor: *One man may eat a pie, but two men can eat three.*"

"How—er, pithy—your majesty."

"Yes, isn't it?" said Markon, and for the first time during this interview, his smile was a real one. "The enchantress is conducting a rather different kind of investigation. I'm sure your two styles can coexist."

"I will not be responsible for any danger the Young Person may find herself in," said the doctor, more stiffly than ever.

"Then I suppose it's just as well I haven't asked you to be responsible for her, isn't it?" said Markon gently. He didn't add that he was quite capable of looking after the young women of the castle because it occurred to him just in time that the trail of bodies and mutilated young women would prove an embarrassing veto. "Wyndsor has been very...*attentive*...in this matter, but I do expect cooperation with anyone else I choose to hire for the job. Thank you for your concern, Doctor."

"I will of course cooperate to the best of *my* ability," said Doctor Romalier, an angry light to his eyes. And then, since he couldn't do anything but accept the dismissal, he bowed short and sharp, and said: "My apologies for interrupting you, your majesty. I shall remove myself."

*Oh, if only!* thought Markon wearily, and went back to his trade papers.

By evening there were two trays of cold food on the occasional table beside Markon's desk, and he had managed to lose the important part of the Avernse/Montalier export proposal. He was engaged in sifting through the mess on his desk when Althea's voice said: "You should try a new filing system."

Markon looked up rather wildly through the sea of paper.

"You know, I'm beginning to wonder why I employ a guard for that staircase."

"Oh, don't worry about that," said Althea. "I noticed your Doctor Romalier slipping past him earlier, so I showed the guard how to look at things from the corners of his eyes. You shouldn't have any more unexpected visitors."

"Yes, but *you're* here," protested Markon. It was obvious that the Avernse/Montalier trade agreement was not going to be finalised today.

"Well, yes. I didn't show him how to stop *me* getting past."

"Of course not!" said Markon. "How can I help you, lady?"

"You should eat more," Althea said. She was looking over the two trays of untouched food. "You're too thin."

"You said I was handsome yesterday," said Markon, forgetting about the trade agreement in pursuance of more interesting topics.

"You are," Althea told him. She tossed him a peach from one of the trays, and took another for herself. Markon found himself eating it because it was there, and discovered that he was really very hungry. "But you need to take care of yourself."

"In Montalier we have a saying," said Markon, enjoying himself.

Althea looked unimpressed. "Does it have anything to do with pies?"

"*The baker of the pies is the last to taste their sweetness,*" Markon continued, ignoring her. He picked through the rest of the cold food and found an apple tart. Fortunately that was *meant* to be cold.

"I thought it might have something to do with pies," Althea said. "Your forebears seem to have had a hearty appetite for them. Not to mention a fascination with dark and dreary tapestries up and down the galleries."

"Speaking of dark and dreary, have you actually met Doctor Romalier?"

"Not in so many words," said Althea, her eyes deepening blue in amusement. "He seemed a bit upset when we er, bumped into each other. I gather he doesn't like sharing his toys. Or maybe he minds who he shares them with. That's not important. What *is* important is that I've found someone for us to talk to."

"Us?"

"I thought you'd like the chance to observe things first hand."

"Yes," said Markon, realising that that was *exactly* what he wanted. He wanted to be away from trade agreements and stuffy international intrigue, and he wanted to tag along with Althea and see exactly what she was up to. "Yes, that's a good idea. How did you find this someone?"

"I took a meal in the upper kitchen," said Althea. "They would have called me out right away in the lower kitchen– that or gone very formal and *m'lady* this and *m'lady* that. But in the upper kitchen they were all very relaxed and easy to talk to. I may have given them the impression that I was a visiting lady's maid."

"Given the impression?"

Althea looked slightly conscious. "Well, I never actually *said* that, but I may have talked about my lady liking her breakfast late, and being impatient with her dressing taking too long. Of course, the talk all came around to the prince's predicament, and one of the girls *almost* said something before she caught herself."

"That's not a lot to go on," said Markon. He'd been hoping for something more certain.

"Nonsense," Althea said. "There's a world of meaning in the almost-saids of the worlds. It's just a matter of making sure you don't take away the wrong almost-said. Besides, she looked frightened of whatever it was she didn't say."

"Who is she?"

"One of your upper housemaids. I understand that she and another girl are in charge of the curtains."

"The curt– what curtains?"

"All of them. Well, all of them except yours and the prince's, of course."

"Do you mean to say that she goes around the castle all day opening and closing curtains?"

Althea nodded. "Apparently there's a rotation. It follows the sun around the castle and makes sure that all the rooms get enough to light them but not enough to ruin the furniture. If a room has guests, the curtains stay open all day. There's a knack to it, Annerlee says."

"Who is Annerlee?"

"She's the girl we're going to see," said Althea, placing her peach pit on Markon's tray. He watched in fascination as she licked her fingers with great solemnity. "You can bring your pie."

"I may have misunderstood the idea of your investigation," said Markon, rising and following her instinctively. "But won't my presence make her *less* likely to talk?"

"It would if you looked like you," Althea said.

"Yes, but I *do* look like me," Markon said, trailing after her as she stepped purposefully from the library and down the hall.

Althea shot him a quick, cautious look that had him wondering what she'd done. "You don't, actually."

She gestured at one of the windows as they passed it, and Markon caught their reflection. Rather to his shock the reflection showed Althea and a stranger dressed in a footman's livery, his long face at the same time familiar and alien. Markon stopped short and took a step toward that traitorous reflection. He wasn't sure he liked the idea of someone being able to do this to him without his knowing.

"I can take it off if you like," said Althea, a troubled line between her brows. "It's just a glamour affecting perception of your face and figure. It's not really changed you."

"No," said Markon thoughtfully, turning his head this way and that to observe the effect. "I didn't expect it, that's all. Perhaps you could warn me first, next time."

"Of course," said Althea. She made a short, sharp turn on the pad of her foot and started energetically down the stairs. Markon thought that she was annoyed with herself.

Annerlee, it turned out, took supper by herself in one of the smaller, sectioned-off courtyards between the north and south wings, a dour figure with unusually long arms and legs and a lapful of small, round rolls that she was methodically spreading with butter from a small handkerchief. She didn't notice them at first, intent upon her rolls, but when she did notice them she looked distinctly worried. Markon got the impression that if she hadn't had a lapful of rolls, she would have tried to skulk away into the shadows that were drawing coolly across the courtyard.

Althea, not one whit dismayed, greeted the other girl with a cheery: "Good evening!"

"'Evening," said Annerlee cautiously. "You're out late, Thea."

"The Lady's having an early night."

"Who's that?"

One of Althea's small hands slipped around Markon's, her fingers threading between his. "This is Mark. He's a footman in the Lady's service. We're, well–"

"Stepping out, eh?" said Annerlee. She looked slightly less nervous.

Markon, jolted out of his surprise by a pinch from Althea's fingers, said: "Since last month," and hoped he looked sufficiently bashful.

"I brought him out to meet you," Althea said chummily.

"Me?" Annerlee looked surprised and not particularly gratified.

"He's awfully interested in the prince's curse, and I told him you were the one to ask about it."

There was no mistaking the rigidity of Annerlee's shoulders. "What do you mean?"

"We heard about the prince's curse in Avernse," said Althea, very carefully oblivious to the other girl's discomfort. "But no one knows very much about it and you said this afternoon that–"

"I'm sorry, you've misunderstood."

"Oh, but–"

"I didn't say anything," said Annerlee, leaping to her feet. Tiny buttered rolls scattered over the flagstones. "I don't know anything! It's none of my business and– I'm late– I–"

She fairly ran away, pushing between them to hurry back to the castle. Althea watched her go with thoughtful eyes, and said: "Now that was interesting."

"And not particularly useful," added Markon.

"Oh no, it's useful," said Althea. "Not as useful as I would have liked, but she obviously knows something about the situation and from what she said yesterday, she knows it's not a curse. I think she knows who's opening Doors into Faery."

"Then how do we get her to talk?"

"That's the easy part," said Althea, turning decidedly back in the direction of the castle. "Let her stew tonight. She's afraid. Tomorrow we'll give her something else to be afraid of, something that scares her so much she *has* to talk."

"What's going to scare her more than she is now?" said Markon sceptically. He'd seen that kind of wide-eyed fear before: it was an unreasoning, unthinking, and above all, self-serving fear.

Althea said: "You are, of course."

## 3

## DAY THREE

"I'm not sure how I feel about this," said Markon. Actually, he was feeling distinctly obstinate. A little of his obstinacy came from the fact that Althea had breezed into his library in a businesslike and wholly impersonal manner to demand his help. She hadn't even said good morning. Adding to that feeling was his dislike of being used as a mallet to force information out of one of his own servants.

"I can *try* to do it myself," said Althea doubtfully. "I'm sure I could come up with something, but I do think it would be better if you did it yourself."

"Better for whom?" demanded Markon.

"Everyone, I suppose," Althea said, taking the question seriously. Her spine was, as usual, entirely straight, and there was an unflinching judgement in her eyes. "Annerlee knows something about the person who killed and mutilated several of your subjects. They deserve your concern first."

"Yes, Nanny," said Markon, which made Althea's eyes widen slightly and then crinkle just as slightly at the corners.

However, all she said was: "If you're ready, your majesty, we can get started."

Unable to resist trying for another sight of those crinkles, Markon said: "All right, but I expect sweeties."

Fifteen minutes later, he was wishing he had never thought of sweeties. Annerlee was lying on the floor of her room with her eyes open and sightless to the ceiling, a whitening of frost coating them and crystal droplets of sweat frozen on her forehead. Blood must at some stage have poured from her ears, eyes, and mouth, but as it came out it had frozen as well, marbles of blood lining the cracks between floorboards and reminding Markon of nothing so much as boiled lollies.

He wished he hadn't thought of sweeties.

"More fae magic," said Althea. There was a tightness to her mouth and Markon made an instinctive movement to usher her from the room again, but she said: "No. We should find out as much as we can before we go."

"What is there to find out?" Markon was pleased to find that his voice sounded merely curious. He'd seen dead people before, of course—killed his share in battle, if it came to that—but this was something different. "She's dead. There's nothing we can do for her."

"I won't be long," said Althea. The crease was back between her brows, deep and sad. Markon wondered if she was thinking of her little sister and the waterfae. He left her to her study of Annerlee and surveyed the room instead. There wasn't much to see: it was about the size of the ablutions chamber in his suite and sparse to the point of being non-descript. It held a bed, a tattered old wardrobe, a curtained-off washing space, and one spindly chair that was coated in enough dust to indicate that it was purely decorative. The only personal thing in the room, in fact, was the lovingly quilted and tatted bedspread that had been half-pulled from the bed, the corner of it still clenched in Annerlee's stiff fingers.

Markon, sick at the futility of the gesture, turned away and took a few restive steps toward the door. Footsteps echoed his, confusing him, and by the time he opened his mouth to say: "I think someone's coming," Althea had already grabbed his hand and was shoving him into the wardrobe.

Markon tried to say: "Why am I hiding from my own subjects?" but all that came out was

"What?" and even that made Althea clap one hand over his mouth in the darkness.

"Quiet," she said in his ear. "I've made us harder to see but if he hears us my little look-away spell won't be much good."

"Why not use a proper hiding spell?" whispered Markon around her hand.

"Big magic is more noticeable than little magic," hissed Althea. "Shush!" Which of course *still* left the question of why he was hiding in a very narrow wardrobe from one of his own people, who by rights should be feeling more awkward about the situation than he.

But when Annerlee's door creaked open and was carefully shut again, it wasn't one of Markon's subjects that he saw through the crack in the wardrobe doors. It was Pilburn, the Wyndsor emissary, his large nostrils quivering and his clever fingers tapping lightly on each surface that he passed.

Markon must have made a soft sound of disbelief, because Althea pressed close to catch a sight of the man through the crack as well. He put his arms around her to prevent them accidentally alighting anywhere that would embarrass both of them, and found himself rethinking his recent dislike of narrow wardrobes. Althea was very still, which might have made him think she was made shy by their proximity if she hadn't already curled her arm around his waist for support, her eye glued to the crack and one small finger, highlighted in the light from the crack, silently *tap-tap-tapping* in a steady, thoughtful rhythm. She was thinking.

When Markon finally turned his thoughts back to Annerlee's room, it was to notice that Pilburn was methodically making his way around the room. He could see the man over Althea's head, gently wiggling stones in the walls to see if they would shift, rapping ceiling beams, and occasionally shifting his weight on the floorboards to tap one foot lightly against them. What was he looking for? Whatever it was, his search would bring him into proximity with the wardrobe before much longer, and Markon began to wonder if Althea's misdirection spell would stand up against this kind of systematic search. Apparently she was wondering the same thing, because as Pilburn drew closer to the wardrobe, Althea's fingers began to trace a complicated pattern on the wardrobe doors.

Markon said, very softly: "Won't he notice?"

Althea finished her tracery before she tiptoed to whisper in his ear: "He's searching physically. He hasn't even got enough magic to light a candle. I thought it would be someone else."

*The Doctor*, thought Markon. *She thought it would be Doctor Romalier. I wonder why?*

She probably thought, as did Markon himself, that it was exceedingly likely Wyndsor was involved in the whole situation. If it proved to be true, Wyndsor could look elsewhere for trade agreements– and think themselves lucky to escape war, if it came to that.

By the time Pilburn, looking confused and a little bit angry, had finished his search of the room, Markon was feeling surprisingly relaxed. Althea, despite her straight spine and general air of businesslike efficiency, was very comfortable to cuddle with and smelled improbably of strawberry shortcake. He found himself irrationally disappointed when Pilburn, with one last, angry look around the room, showed himself out, prompting Althea to disengage herself and softly open the wardrobe door again.

Markon, somewhat slower to remove himself from the wardrobe, murmured: "What do you think he was looking for?"

"That's what I'd like very much to know," said Althea. She was frowning down at the floorboards, deep in thought. "I'd also like to know how he knew Annerlee was dead. He didn't murder her– or at least, not personally. This is High Fae magic; Unseelie, I think. He did come looking for something in particular, though, and that's rather curious."

"Perhaps I should call Pilburn and Doctor Romalier in for an interview," said Markon.

"Oh no!" said Althea, looking up at once. "Please don't! Doctor Romalier is making things difficult at the moment, and I'm interested in *what* he makes difficult. At the moment I'm not sure if he's deliberately trying to keep something from me, or if he simply doesn't want me getting into his investigation. I'll be certain in a day or two."

"What, then?"

"May I?"

Markon looked at her uncomprehendingly: blinked. "Oh! Of course! Where are we going this time?"

"The kitchen, first. I'll use the same glamour for you as yesterday. Then it might be a good idea to announce my er, candidacy to the court."

"Are we still walking out together?"

Althea appeared to give this some serious thought. "No; on the whole, I think it'd be better for you to go in first. You can still be my lady's footman, though. Find somewhere nice and shadowy to sit: somewhere you can see everyone but not everyone can see you."

"You want me to watch for reactions," said Markon approvingly.

Althea gave him a conspiratorial nod. "Someone knew that Annerlee knew too much. I'd guess they saw us talking to her as well, and that's why they took fright. It's more likely to be someone from the kitchens, but I think it's time we stirred things up around court, too."

Markon, refusing to commit himself to stirring things up in a manner that was likely to see Althea murdered, said: "What about the poor girl's body?"

"I think it might be best if someone else discovers it," said Althea.

It was ridiculous to feel so nervous about an excursion into the upper kitchens. All of these people were his subjects, after all. But between entering the room as His Royal Majesty King Markon of Montalier and Attached Islands, and entering the room as a visiting lady's footman, was a vast and uncomfortable difference. Much to his relief, he was barely given a glance when he entered. The cook gave him a fat, absent smile and a full bowl of hearty stew, and one of the castle footmen said a pleasant: "Afternoon! New, eh?" as he slipped into a greasy seat by the coal scuttle; but otherwise he was paid very little attention. With his back to the chimney, its front facade shielding him from both its direct heat and light, he was really very easy to overlook. Markon was grateful for that: he hadn't felt this out of place since his coronation, the only other time he'd expected people to stand up and point accusing fingers at him while howling: *"Imposter!"*

The chatter that went on around the kitchen tables was vaguely cyclic and while it was interesting it wasn't exactly helpful. Every so often one group would finish up and leave, only for another to take its place with conversational variations upon the same themes of the prince, the curse, which footman was stepping out with which maid, and speculations upon the visiting enchantress– of whom, Markon was amused to notice, they had not seen a hair, but were buzzing with information regardless.

Althea herself didn't make an appearance for some time. In fact, Markon was beginning to wonder if she'd found something else to occupy her by the time she arrived. Her arrival caused significantly more notice than his own had done: several of the kitchen staff hailed her with cheerfully impolite remarks, and the cook paused from her pots and spits for long enough to beam at her. Even some of the upper maids were pleased to smile at her from their lofty height of superiority. Althea took a place not too high and not too low along the table and accepted the bowl that she was given, surprising Markon by the ease with which she fit into the group. His experience of enchantresses had made him very aware of the importance they attached to themselves, and their certainty of being equal with the highest in the land, royalty notwithstanding. Althea evidently applied the same approach to other levels of society: she certainly didn't seem to find herself anything but equal with the upper kitchen staff. They, on their part, were soon chattering away again as if they'd never stopped, and Markon sat back against the chimney with his empty bowl clasped comfortably in his hands, watching and listening.

They had moved on to discussing the guests at the castle before Althea did anything but eat and listen. Then, she said: "That doctor's a pushy one, isn't he?"

There were several knowing smirks and one contemptuous snort from an upper maid who should have been above such a noise.

"Investigating the prince's curse, he is," said one of the footmen. "Important old buzzard, ain't he?"

"Self-important, more like," said the upper maid who had snorted.

"Nan's in the right," said one of the kitchen maids. "I heard him say as how it had to be a woman that put the curse on him. Said they were all spiteful-like, the accidents, and it must have been a woman that done 'em."

Althea looked rather amused. "Is that so? I suppose that accounts for the questions he flung at the scullery maid this morning."

One of the footmen said wrathfully: "If he's been upsetting Betsy again, I'll have a few words to say to the steward about it!"

"Oh well, at least it's not another girl," said a kitchen maid. "It's a cryin' shame, all those dead girls. The curse ain't gonna harm him, now is it?"

"We can only hope!" said the footman.

Althea sipped tea thoughtfully. "So no one else is willing to try and break the curse?"

"Such a shame!" said one of the upper maids. "It's so romantic! Imagine being married to the prince!"

"Imagine breaking every bone in your body or being boiled on the inside while being frozen from the outside," retorted the maid called Nan. "You imagine *that*, Cinna! Anyway, it's not romantic, it's disgusting. One little floozy after another trying to force her way into the royal family."

"Jumped up little trollops," agreed another voice. "Why should they think themselves good enough for the prince, I'd like to know! Who are they? Who are their families?"

"I still think it's romantic," said Cinna. "None of this hoity-toity *them and us*: it's a chance for any girl to make a name for herself." Again there was that snort of derision, but the little maid pressed on, undeterred: "What's more, Nan, if I wasn't such a coward I'd try for myself, so I would! Just think! To be queen!"

"What about the enchantress that's visiting?" said a kitchen maid, setting a fresh plate of bread on the table. "Do you think she's trying for the prince? She'd have a good chance, that one."

One or two curious pairs of eyes turned toward Althea, who was still sipping tea, and the upper maid called Nan said: "You're maid to one of the guests, aren't you? Is the enchantress your mistress? You didn't say."

"Oh no!" said Althea, in a friendly fashion. "I'm the enchantress. I'm here to break the curse."

4
---

## DAY FOUR

*T*hat girl! thought Markon. That headstrong, careless little imp of trouble and worry, should be thoroughly shaken! He'd gone to bed with his annoyance and woken with it still fresh in his mind. He hadn't intended to tell the whole court that Althea was there to break Parrin's 'curse', but once she'd told the staff in the upper kitchen, it didn't really matter *what* he'd meant to do. The story would be around the castle faster than the smell in a slaughterhouse on a hot day. What was worse was that he'd not heard from Althea all morning. He hadn't been able to get to his library, either, since midweek was always set aside for Hearings until at least noon. Anyone suing for justice or appealing for a pardon could apply to the castle and be seen on midweek day: a task which Markon usually found interesting if not particularly heartening. Today it seemed long, tortuous, and particularly galling.

His annoyance simmered all through the midweek hearings and flared again when Althea didn't show up in the library to report at noon either. Annerlee's body had just been discovered when he left the midweek hearings, and though Markon had already known about it, the reminder was unpleasant– lying to his seneschal about it more so. When that interview was at last finished he hurried to the library again, only to find it still empty of Althea. What was she up to *now*?

Markon had just sat down in some irritation to eat a light, late lunch when his steward knocked on the door to announce that Doctor Romalier would like to see him on a matter of some urgency.

Anticipating Markon's curt denial of any wish to see the doctor, his steward added: "I understand it has something to do with the curse, your majesty. I believe it may be important."

Markon checked the impatient retort that rose to his lips and after a moment's fed-up silence, said with a faint smile: "All right. Show him in."

But when Doctor Romalier entered, he was not alone. Markon, who wouldn't have been surprised to see Pilburn the emissary with him, *was* surprised to see one of his own court magicians with the Doctor. Doctor Fenke, his venerable old beard jutting with as much importance as Doctor Romalier's, nevertheless looked unusually worried.

Both men bowed and discreetly waited for Markon's steward to close the door. Then Fenke said solemnly: "Your majesty, Doctor Romalier has apprised me of a serious situation. A very serious situation indeed."

"That's very kind of him," said Markon, looking from Fenke's important, serious face to Romalier's important, smug one. "Was it something he felt uncomfortable discussing with me?"

"Not uncomfortable, your majesty," said Doctor Romalier smoothly; "But as a guest here I felt that your majesty would prefer to have a Montalieran opinion as well."

"A Montalieran opinion on *what*, exactly?" Markon demanded. He felt that the day would have been less irritating had he simply stayed in bed, where he could have had the felicity of brooding over Althea's wrongdoing in peace.

"During my investigations this morning, I chanced to come

across some rather clever monitoring magic," said Romalier. Incredibly, he seemed to be getting smugger by the minute. "It's a style I often see used in espionage work, your majesty: a listening spell placed somewhere of interest and trailing back somewhere that the magic user can hide away and listen at will."

"I see," said Markon slowly. He was beginning to have a very bad feeling about this, and it wasn't because of the espionage magic. This smelled for all the world like a setup. "Where was the listening spell placed?"

"We've just now traced it here to your library," said Doctor Fenke apologetically. "As a matter of fact, I can see it over *there*, your majesty. It's webbed up behind your desk."

Markon threw an instinctive glance over his shoulder, but didn't really expect to see anything. Nor did he. "Can you dismantle it?" he asked.

"Of course," said Doctor Fenke.

Doctor Romalier, smoother than ever, suggested: "Surely it's best to follow it to its source first, your majesty?"

Markon looked at the Doctor for a long thoughtful minute before he said: "Lead the way. I'll come with you."

He wasn't at all surprised when the two Doctors led him directly to Althea's suite. If it had been anyone but Doctor Fenke —old, set in his ways and entirely honourable, if slightly stick-in-the-mud-ish—Markon would have suspected that Doctor Romalier had paid for his second opinion. As it was, he could do nothing but tell his steward, whom he had also brought along with the distinct suspicion that he would be needed, to fetch Althea from whichever part of the castle she was presently occupying.

"Bring her courteously," he added. His steward, with the gleam of intelligence in his eye that had caused Markon to appoint him in the first place, nodded.

"Your majesty, what if she escapes?" said Doctor Romalier in dismay. "Surely a squad of guards in magic-resistant armour would be more appropriate!"

"Appropriate for what, exactly?" enquired Markon gently. "Starting a war with Avernse? Dishonouring a lady who has had nothing proved against her as yet?"

Doctor Romalier huffed a little, and at last said: "Will you not enter the room, your majesty? What are we waiting for?"

"We're waiting for the enchantress," said Markon, more gently still. "We're showing ourselves to be gentlemen and not boors. When the lady hears the charges she'll let us in without reservation."

Both doctors looked dubious, but neither dared to say any more. This happy state of silence continued until Markon's steward appeared once again, Althea a step behind him and walking swiftly. There was a gleam of interest in her eyes that turned to wariness when she saw the two doctors beside Markon, and he fancied he saw them narrow slightly.

"I understand you wish to speak with me, your majesty," she said formally, curtseying.

Markon saw Doctor Romalier open his mouth to speak, and said quickly: "Doctors Romalier and Fenke have discovered an espionage spell in my library that leads back to your rooms. I told them that you'd be happy to open your suite to us in order to clear yourself."

"And so I am," said Althea, though he thought she looked rather shocked. Her eyes weren't on the floor, but he was certain that she was thinking very quickly indeed. She opened the doors for them, her eyes following the same line of sight as the two doctors, and all three of them gazed in silence at the dressing table across the room, where Althea's combs were set out.

"You see?" said Doctor Romalier in triumph. "The spell is grounded in that comb! What have you to say for yourself, enchantress?"

Althea studied the comb in silence, and Markon wondered if it was just his imagination, or if she really had grown paler.

"Well?" demanded Doctor Romalier. "Well, enchantress?"

"Steady on, Romalier," protested Doctor Fenke uncomfortably. "Give the enchantress a chance to breathe."

Markon, with a sour edge of dismay beginning to curl in his stomach, said: "Can you explain this spell, lady?"

"Certainly," said Althea. There was a lightness to her blue eyes that Markon wasn't familiar with, and he wasn't quite sure what it meant. "This isn't human magic, Doctors. It's fae magic. But don't take my word for it: see for yourselves."

Doctor Romalier's eyes bulged. "What? That's impossible!"

Doctor Fenke, fumbling eagerly with a pair of circular, ground-glass spectacles, said excitedly: "I never would have thought to check! Egads! She's right, Romalier! Look at this!"

"I can see perfectly well from here, thank you!" snapped Doctor Romalier, fending off the comb as Doctor Fenke thrust it under his nose.

"Fancy that! Fae magic! Who would have thought, eh? Well, this certainly clears the enchantress of any wrongdoing, I'm glad to say."

"Thank you, Doctor," said Althea primly.

"On the other hand, it opens up a rather more dangerous proposition," remarked Doctor Fenke. He didn't look as though the prospect was unpleasant: Markon got the distinct impression that he was still immensely excited. "It seems that you've got a fae running around your court, your majesty."

"Come now, it's a little previous to be making that sort of judgement!" protested Doctor Romalier. "A fae in the Montalieran Court?"

"Doctor Romalier," interrupted Markon; "I assume that you've also absolved the lady of all wrong-doing?"

"Well, in a manner of speaking– it does seem that– and if it really *is* fae magic–"

"It is!" said Doctor Fenke in surprise. "You can see it as well as I can, man! Can't think why we didn't check in the first place."

"Well, I don't really see how the enchantress *can* be responsible," said Doctor Romalier reluctantly.

"Thank you *so* much," said Althea. "Would you all mind if I dismantle it now? I'm rather uncomfortable with it being here in my room."

"Go ahead, go ahead," Doctor Fenke said affably. "I'd very much like to see you work, lady." But Althea's eyes had flicked up to meet Markon's, and it wasn't until he nodded that she took the comb from a sulky Doctor Romalier, whose assent was also grudgingly given.

Doctor Romalier may have been grudging, and he may have been outspoken in his dismissal of enchantresses in general and Althea in particular, but Markon noticed that he watched her with narrowed eyes for the entire operation. To Markon it seemed as though all Althea did was scrape the back of her thumbnail against the tines of the comb, back and forth, back and forth: but the two Doctors were spell-bound.

When Althea said: "There we go," and tossed the comb back onto her dressing-table, all three of them jumped, each of them to some extent mesmerised.

Doctor Fenke was the first to recover himself. He said: "Well, if that's all, I think we've trespassed on your good nature long enough. That was a first-class unworking, madam! First class!"

"Not at all inferior," said Doctor Romalier coldly. "I'll walk with you, Fenke."

They withdrew together, leaving Markon and his steward to hear Althea's sudden: "Well, that's interesting! You'd probably better stay."

"What's interesting?" asked Markon, indicating to his very surprised steward that he could leave. The man did so, his face struggling between proper reserve and faint approval.

"The espionage magic isn't the only fae magic in the room."

"What?"

"Someone—some fae—has dropped a very nasty bit of magic on my bedside rug," said Althea.

"No, don't come closer, for all I know it could be a sticky one. Throw me an apple, will you?"

"Hungry, are you?" said Markon dryly, but he threw her one of the apples from the fruit bowl by the window. "What are you— oh."

Althea tossed the apple into the centre of the rug from a careful distance, a flash of red against blue that changed to a flash of cream against blue and then shattered in a cascade of porcelain apple shards.

"Not very nice," said Althea, observing the mess. "Still, that seems to have gotten rid of it, so it can't have been a very high level fae."

"I'll have you changed into a different suite," said Markon tightly. "If you hadn't—"

"If I hadn't stirred things up, I wouldn't have to change suites?"

Exasperatedly, Markon said: "You wouldn't be in danger!"

"Yes, but just think! There were two different kinds of nasty magic in my suite. *Two.* Unless we're dealing with a very disturbed person, it seems obvious that in *this* situation at least—"

"—there are two people involved."

"Exactly," said Althea, smiling at him. "One of them wants to implicate me in espionage; another wants to make it look like I've been taken by the curse as well."

"What else did you get up to today?" asked Markon, sitting down absentmindedly on Althea's plump couch. Rather to his disappointment she didn't join him: she sat on the bed instead, her back as straight as ever but her arms folded comfortably on the footboard.

"I was looking for Doors," she said. "Nothing to make anyone try to discredit me via espionage. And honestly, I don't think it was Doctor Romalier, either."

"Don't you?" said Markon. "I'm not so sure."

"Well, neither am I, if it comes to that. And he was awfully angry when he found out it was fae magic instead of human."

"But that could just be Romalier being the pleasant human being he is," nodded Markon, following the thought that Althea had left unsaid. A blaze of *what if* flashed across his mind, and he added slowly: "Or it could be that someone *told* him what to expect, and he felt that he'd been made a fool of. He was certain that the magic would be yours."

"He was, wasn't he?" said Althea, after the barest possible pause. "That's an interesting possibility. Oh! How odd: one of my combs is missing."

"The one that was used in the espionage magic?"

"No. It's a set of three. One is still missing: my favourite."

Markon, unsure if he should be commiserating or grasping a point, said: "Who took it?"

"Well, that's the question," she said. "Things like combs are usually taken because of what they have more than because of what they are."

"You think they wanted your hair," said Markon, after far too long in thought.

Althea gave him a pleased little nod that made him feel he'd been particularly clever. "Exactly. I think that's how the victims are being targeted. Which brings me to the issue of Doors between here and Faery."

"Did you find any useful ones?"

"Not useful so much as interesting," said Althea thoughtfully. "You won't like it, I'm afraid."

"Won't like what?"

"There are quite a few Doors through to Faery around the castle. At least one for every girl that was injured or killed or taken. Someone has been opening them quite regularly. The ones

I found are mostly dormant or dead by now, but a few are still active, and even the dead and dormant ones weaken the barriers between here and there."

Markon's breath hissed between his teeth. "You mean eventually fae could come through uninvited?"

"Yes. Whoever is bringing fae through and attacking these girls doesn't understand the danger of what they're doing."

"Where were the Doors?" asked Markon. It occurred to him that very few people in the court had access to *all* of the castle; similarly, the servants were contained in their paths of back stairs and serviced rooms, each set occupying its own orbit. The position of the Doors might prove useful in determining to which particular set of people the perpetrator belonged.

Althea gave him a sharp, considering look. "That's a very good question," she said. "I'll look more particularly this afternoon to be sure. Most of them seem to be in the middle of the castle: guest rooms and unused galleries in the courtiers' apartments. Some of them are on back stairways that are mostly for the servants, and there are even two in the courtyards. None outside the castle as far as I've been able to tell."

"Then it's almost certainly a daily occupant of the castle itself," said Markon, a little bitterly. Oddly enough, he would rather have thought that Wyndsor was responsible.

Althea nodded. "Perhaps I can narrow it down to servant or courtier by this afternoon. Regardless–"

"You're going into Faery."

"I think it's best. I can only narrow it down so far from this side. Courtier or servant, there are hundreds to choose between."

"Don't forget–"

"I won't leave you behind," said Althea in a friendly fashion. "But I'll have to find a viable Door first: I'd rather not open another if I can avoid it, and we'll be taking fae magic through with us as it is. No need to complicate matters more than we have to. Simple is best when it comes to fae magic."

"Why will we be taking fae magic through with us?"

"I'd like to find the fae that the different spells belong to. If I can scrape together enough from one of the girls, I should be able to take us exactly where we need to go."

"Do we really *want* to find the sort of fae who can simultaneously burn someone from the inside and freeze them from the outside?"

"That's what I'm for," said Althea, a rather formidable look sitting oddly on her pointed little face. "I'm as dangerous as most of the fae over there."

MARKON WAS DRAGGED FROM DEEP, restful slumber some time after midnight. Someone was prodding his shoulder with irritating regularity, and their persistence was quickly driving away his ability to sleep. Snarling, Markon sat up in bed to find that Althea was sitting beside him.

"How did you get in here?" he groaned.

"I am *very* good at what I do," Althea said primly. "Are you ready?"

"Ready for what?"

"I've found us a live Door into Faery."

# 5

## DAY FIVE

"We're going now?"

"Of course. I'll wait outside."

Markon almost flopped back onto his pillows and went to sleep again. Fortunately, it occurred to him just in time that Althea would only go without him if he did so, and with further mutterings he dragged himself out of bed and into yesterday's clothes again.

By the time he was dressed Markon's sluggish thoughts had begun to work a little less sluggishly, and once outside his suite he was able to ask quite intelligently if Althea had managed to collect the fae magic she needed.

"More than enough," said Althea. Unlike Markon, who was looking rather wrinkled but carelessly opulent, she was dressed in rich autumn colours that were not only expensive but beautiful. An air of distant nobility sat on her face, and he thought that she carried herself differently tonight than she had earlier. He was certain of it when she turned and glided down the hall ahead of him. Where was her bouncing, energetic walk? Tonight she looked unapproachable and regal and not quite human. How long exactly had Althea spent in Faery, alone and lost in an alien land?

Althea said: "Are you coming?" and Markon, realising that he'd been staring after her, spurred himself into motion again.

Markon couldn't see the Door: but then, he hadn't expected to see it. According to Althea, it was directly opposite them in one dark corner of a quiet library in the west wing of the castle. She was doing small, invisible things in preparation, her eyes shadowed and impossible to read in the darkness. Markon heard the sound of the internal clock striking the quarter past twelve in delicate bells before she seemed to be finished. He still couldn't see the Door. He had begun to wonder if Althea had done something wrong when she made a decided motion with one hand, as though opening an invisible door, and Markon found that he could see it very clearly indeed. It was a rectangle of bright, warm sunshine that should have lit and warmed the midnight library but didn't seem to quite touch it. A vibrantly green summer leaf wafted through the Door, floating on a warm breeze that faintly touched Markon's face, and once his eyes adjusted to the light he could see the green and gold forest from which it came, ruffled lightly in the wind and too beautiful to be real.

"Are you ready?" asked Althea, her face white and expressionless in the oddly cold sunlight.

"No," said Markon, but Althea had him by the hand and was already pulling him irresistibly into the untouchable beauty of Faery. Markon couldn't resist looking over his shoulder, quick and fearful. Behind them was more of the same beautiful forest, as gold and green and untouchably gorgeous as that around them, and in it there was a slight crack.

"It's still open," Althea said. Here in Faery her eyes seemed bluer, her face even paler; and when she moved, her skirts rippling like the leaves in the trees above them, she looked almost fae. Beside her, Markon felt heavy and earthy and very, very human. "I left a kind of doorstopper in it," she added. "It won't close until we go back through."

"What if something else gets through?"

"Nothing will get through," said Althea firmly.

"It doesn't feel real here," Markon said. His neck crawled with the feeling of being watched, and the too-perfect forest around them seemed to shift and move in his periphery. "And it's daylight. Why is it daylight?"

"We've come in to a Seelie piece of Faery. It's always daylight here: a forever of sun and summer with just tiny bits of autumn and spring at the edges. If we'd come into an Unseelie piece it would be all sable and moonlight and starlight. Do you feel like you're being watched?" she added suddenly.

"Yes!" said Markon gratefully.

"It's your mind trying to come to grips with all of this," said Althea, making an unconsciously graceful gesture at the grandeur around them. "Our bodies are different to *theirs*. The sunshine never seems to sink in further than skin-deep with us, and sometimes you can be convinced for years at a time that it's all a dream and nothing is real. They don't like coming through to our world much, either. They like the games, but they're always trying to change the world to suit themselves and not all of them have the power to keep trying. That's why they make quick little dashes out to steal children and play pranks. You'll feel more comfortable after a while, but it never quite goes away."

"How long were you here?" asked Markon, eyeing the resplendent trees in some dislike.

"Oh, about eighteen years," said Althea. She was looking away through the trees, as if trying to get her bearings. "The trace on our fae magic leads this way. We should be as quick as we can."

"Eighteen years!" Markon hurried to catch up with her, his heavy feet sinking into the forest floor of moss and fallen leaves. He couldn't imagine living with this creeping feeling of not-quite-reality for eighteen years.

"Eighteen that I remember," Althea said shortly. "It's probably best if you don't let them know you're royalty. Royalty is very useful to them, and some fae like to collect kings."

"That's appalling," said Markon, abandoning the attempt to draw more information from her. Her time in Faery was obviously not something that she wanted to talk about.

"Don't worry," said Althea, with the ghost of a smile on her lips; "I won't let them keep you."

The forest began to thin out soon after they started walking, grand, aged trees giving way to slender young saplings that were more sparsely spaced. A clearing, or an end to the forest? Markon wondered, looking up to catch a glimpse of the sky. It was high and delightfully blue, with perfect, pearly clouds scattered across it in the most aesthetically pleasing manner. Like the rest of Faery, it had the effect of making him feel heavy, human, and vaguely grubby. He couldn't help feeling that it was just a little bit *too* bright: a little bit *too* beautiful.

Althea, lightly touching his arm, said: "It's best not to look at it for too long," and Markon found to his surprise that he'd stopped walking. "In our world there's the idea of moon-madness," she said, curling her fingers through the crook of his arm as if they were merely out for a stroll. "Here it doesn't matter whether it's the moon or the clouds, if you look up at the sky for too long you start to see strange things."

"I'm beginning to think that this is a rather bad idea," said Markon, but he was amused and a little interested to see that Althea with her hand tucked in his arm was closer to the bouncing, energetic Althea of the human world than she had been just a little while ago. It made him feel less worried, which brought him to the realisation that he'd been worrying about her in the first place.

"Well, yes," said Althea. "But it was the best idea out of a slew of worse ones. Is that a cottage, do you think?"

It *was* a cottage: the sight of which, much to Markon's disappointment, caused Althea to withdraw her hand and become distant and fae-like once again. She consulted a vague webbing of *something* that glittered between her fingers and gave a decisive nod. "This is it," she said. "Don't be goaded into insulting the fae, and try to avoid making anything that could be construed as a promise."

"You mean try not to talk if I can help it," said Markon, and was rewarded by the brief crinkling of Althea's eyes. She knocked at the door with one firm little fist, eschewing the iron knocker—which, now that Markon thought about it, was a very odd thing for a fae to have on their front door. Althea's eyes met his over her shoulder and the faint amusement in them told him all he needed to know: the iron knocker was there to announce a particular type of caller. A fae would never use an iron knocker—*couldn't* use one—which meant that the fae inside would know the moment a human caller appeared at his or her door. Which begged the question, thought Markon, growing cold: just how many human visitors had this particular fae encountered before it seemed expedient to mount an iron knocker on the door?

The door opened while he was still wondering about it. The elderly fae who had opened it stared at them with piercing golden eyes, two rather cruel lines appearing by the sides of a smile that would otherwise have been quite pleasant. She said: "You're an interesting pair."

"I found something that belongs to you," said Althea, just as abruptly.

The fae turned her head curiously, and the lines by her mouth deepened in a sharper curl of the lips. "Kind of you to bring it all this way. You must come in."

"Thank you," said Althea, following her into the house. Markon followed them both, wondering why it was that the fae's hospitality made him feel *more* nervous instead of less.

"Your human doesn't talk much," the fae said, bringing them into a tiny sitting room. A dedicated sitting room seemed out of place in such a small cottage, but Markon got the feeling that the fae liked to think herself very fine. That feeling helped him to meet her golden eyes and stare wordlessly at her until she looked away first, cackling.

"He learns slowly, but he learns well," said Althea, curling the hairs on the back of Markon's neck with the coldness of her voice.

The fae grinned sharply. "I see that. You've bought me something that I'll be glad to have back, but I'm curious to know how you got it: I left it in a place that is hard to find."

"The human world," nodded Althea. "I know."

"What led you to bring it back to me?"

"I'm in need of information," said Althea. "Someone is interfering with a matter that concerns me, and I'd like to know who."

The fae's sharp old eyes became watchful. "Didn't seek to cross you, lady. There was a debt to be paid. I paid it in service and was let in once the spell was prepared." There was an undercurrent of bitterness in her harsh voice, Markon was certain. Whatever the 'debt' was that she had paid, she had not paid it happily.

"To whom did you owe this debt?"

"Human scum," said the fae, and this time the bitterness was stronger. "No name given, merely a few hairs and a way through. Simple matter of a debt to be paid. I'll be glad to have the magic back, however."

"Male or female?"

"Never saw a face," she said shortly. "And the voice wasn't distinctive. I'm one that knows how to pay my debts. I keep my head down and do what's needed."

Althea let the silence draw out until the fae's eyes dropped again. Then she said: "I see."

Markon didn't see anything physical pass between the two of them: perhaps a glitter in the air, nothing more. But the fae said: "Thanks, lady," and Althea nodded.

"My thanks for your information," she said formally. To Markon, she said: "Come, human. Our business is done here."

"How did you come by my cottage?" asked the fae, her eyes suddenly sly again. "Did you come from the world of men?"

"I came from my home," Althea said. "We'll not trespass upon your hospitality any longer."

"Can't blame an old fae for being curious," said the fae, with a not very convincing chuckle.

The fae saw them to the door and no further, but Markon wasn't surprised when Althea set out in an entirely different direction to the one they'd come.

"My skin is still crawling," he said softly. "Is she following us?"

"Almost certainly," said Althea, and he was relieved to hear the warmth of her voice. "I'm sorry I had to talk to you like that back there, but most fae don't understand anything except a slave and master relationship between fae and human."

"I didn't take offense," said Markon. He kept his voice low, fearful of being overheard, but couldn't resist adding: "She thought you're a fae. Why?"

Althea's eyes, dark blue as she glided through the shadows of the forest, said: "I told you. I'm very good at what I do."

"I'm beginning to understand that," Markon said. "What will we do next?"

"Harvest more magic to trace, I think," said Althea. "She was holding back something important. It might help to compare her story with the stories of other fae."

Markon found himself smiling at her single-mindedness. "I meant what will we do now? If she's following us, we can't go back to the Door."

"Oh, that. So long as we get there first and shut it behind us, she can't follow us. Still, we'll lead her about for a bit and hope she becomes weary of following us."

Althea walked them through the forest until Markon no longer cared if the fae was following or not. His legs were hurting, his lower back was wet with sweat, and the only thing he could think about apart from his bed was a refreshing wash in his ablutions chamber. He might have broken and complained like a travel-weary child if he hadn't at last recognised a few familiar formations of trees and realised that they were very close to where they'd stepped into Faery.

Althea said: "Wait here, please," and took a few steps forward. By now used to obeying her, Markon stayed where he was and watched the swift, economical motions she made with her hands. He wished he could see what it was she was really doing.

He was so caught up in those delicate movements that it wasn't until Althea said: "Markon," that he recalled his surroundings. It was the deliberate, careful usage of his name that made him really pay attention. Althea's back was still to him, but she said crisply: "Duck *now*, please."

Markon dropped to his haunches while she was still speaking, and felt the swish of something rather hefty sweep over his head. Then Althea wasn't in front of him anymore, and a brief, violent struggle was taking place directly behind him. It was all over in the miniscule amount of time that it took him to turn, still crouched. To his vast amusement, Althea was sitting on the old fae, twisting up one scrawny arm behind the fae's back without deference to her age. Beside them in the fallen leaves was a good sturdy walking stick that had just whistled over his head in an attempt to knock Markon out, if he wasn't mistaken.

He heard Althea say, very softly: "If you try to hurt my human again, I will flay the skin from your body and use it as a rain duster."

"Mercy!" squealed the fae, her skinny legs wriggling. "Mercy, lady! Wouldn't have killed him, I just wanted to come through!"

"A stick!" said Althea, her voice thick with scorn. "You really did need that magic, didn't you?"

"Wouldn't really have hurt him! Just quieted him and sold him on."

"Oh, be quiet!" Althea said, with a pinching motion. The fae abruptly stopped talking, though Markon would have been willing to bet that she did so only because Althea had laid a spell on her. "And be still! You will not be free to move until we are gone from Faery. Be silent. Be still."

"Are you going to leave her like that?" said Markon, his eyes dancing.

Althea stood up, smoothing her hair and tugging her bodice straight again. "Yes, and serve her right if a passing will'o'the'whisp decides to dance on her nose until she can move again! She won't bother us now. If I'd known how little magic she really had left to her I would have left her locked in the cottage."

"That would have been a pity," Markon said, despite aching legs, sweaty clothes and general tiredness. "I wouldn't have missed that little scuffle for the world! Who taught you how to twist an arm like that?"

For a brief moment Althea looked taken aback, and Markon was afraid that he'd accidentally stirred more unpleasant memories. Then she laughed; a real, amused chuckle of mirth that warmed him from head to toe, and said: "They taught me that at Holbrooks when I was studying to become an enchantress. The Head said that magic isn't always reliable and that sometimes a well-placed punch can do more than a spell."

"I'm inclined to think the Head was right," said Markon, with a last, amused look at the prone fey. She gave him a glare with her golden eyes that made him step rather more quickly to Althea's side, grateful that the Door now seemed to be well and truly open. It was achingly good to see the darkened interior of the castle.

MARKON SLEPT ONLY a little later than usual that morning despite the fact that he didn't get back to his room until it was already early morning. He might have slept in longer if he hadn't gone to bed in his sticky, leafy clothes and woken just as sticky and uncomfortable a little after his normal rising time. Markon stripped himself hastily before he rang for his valet, disposing of the worst of the Faery leaves out the window, where they danced away in a rather curious manner. They seemed to chase the wind, joyfully tumbling in the early morning sunlight.

Markon left them to flit away any way they would and then rang for his valet, who brought with him a fresh set of underclothes, outerclothes, and the intelligence that Doctor Romalier wished to complain about the enchantress.

"He can complain to my steward," said Markon firmly, rubbing his hair dry with his facecloth much to the valet's dismay. "What is it this time?"

"He claims that she's been encouraging the female staff to, well, make snide remarks when he questions them," said the valet, trying not to laugh.

Markon grinned. "*Has* she, now?"

"He also claims that she's been interfering with the surveillance magic he set up with your permission. He says that the recorded data has been tampered with."

"I suppose it's too much to expect that he has any proof?"

"No, your majesty," said the valet cheerfully. "Just hot air!"

"That settles it," said Markon. "He *can* complain to my steward. I'll be in my library, working on trade agreements and not to be disturbed."

When Markon got to the library Althea was already there. Much to his amusement, she was fast asleep on his fattest armchair, her cheek resting on the plump red armrest and her head cradled in one arm. The other arm had dropped over the side of the chair, lost in the folds of her skirt, and her feet were curled up beside her. The russet-red of the armchair showed up the paleness of her face and the smudges beneath her eyes, so Markon left her to sleep instead of waking her to mendaciously demand if she was leaving Faery dirt on his chairs from her shoes. It would have been a more pleasant past-time, but Althea needed the sleep and the trade agreements wouldn't revise themselves, after all. He resolutely sat down at his desk and forced himself to concentrate on the papers, and when lunch came and went without Althea doing more than stirring vaguely and muttering in her sleep, he shook off the languor that always came with a morning spent hunched over papers, and went to fetch his own lunch. He could have had it brought into the library, but his legs needed the stretching and Althea looked as though she was likely to sleep for a while longer anyway.

There were voices issuing from the library when Markon returned. He'd brought a tray with him, dismissing the footman who would have carried it for him, with the unformed idea that the smell of it might waken Althea– and that waking, she would be bound to be hungry. To hear voices, therefore, was something of a surprise. Markon halted and listened: that was Parrin's voice, of course, readily recognisable. After it came Althea's, friendly and pleasant. The library door was already ajar, so he shouldered it open and trod softly into the room with his tray.

Althea was no longer on the fat little armchair she'd been sleeping in: instead, she was sitting close to Parrin on the loveseat by the window, both of them leaning forward slightly, both of them engrossed in their conversation. When they saw Markon, the conversation stopped abruptly and each of them sat back a little. Parrin's face looked distinctly conscious, and even Althea looked slightly taken pink: they were the very picture of lovers interrupted.

*And let that be a salutary lesson to you*, thought Markon bitterly to himself. *She's at least fifteen years younger than you and she's promised to Parrin. Keep your mind on breaking the curse.*

Aloud, he said: "Hungry, children?"

"I should think so!" said Parrin eagerly. Markon couldn't help feeling somewhat sardonic. The boy was fond of food, it was true, but his powers of misdirection and concealment hadn't improved since childhood and it was far too easy to see that he was merely trying to divert his father's attention from the somewhat intimate setting in which he and Althea had been found.

Althea, it seemed, was rather more sincere in her acceptance of the food Markon had brought. Not only did she eat more of it than Parrin did, she also failed entirely to notice that he'd left the library while she was solemnly engaged in choosing comfits from the silver-and-pearl box of sweetmeats. When she did notice that he'd gone, all she said was: "We may as well get on with it, then."

Markon, filching the box of sweetmeats before she could eat all of them, said: "Get on with what?"

"Planning, of course," said Althea seriously. "Didn't I tell you? No, I fell asleep before you got here. I pulled more fae magic from the infirmary: it's led me to another usable Door into Faery."

6

## DAY SIX

*T*here was someone sitting next to him on the bed. Markon's breath hissed between his teeth, one hand on its way to grasp his assailant's throat before he realised that it was only Althea. Markon's hand dropped back to the bed and then dug through his rumpled hair as he huffed his relief into the darkness of the room.

"I'm beginning to think Doctor Romalier is right," he told her.

Althea, who hadn't so much as flinched at his instinctive lunge to attack, tilted her head and said: "Really? I wouldn't have thought it was very likely."

"He says that you're a disrupting influence and a drain on the monarch's resources."

Althea gave her low, delighted chuckle. "I suppose it's true, really! A case of the cherry tart calling the raspberry red, though, isn't it?"

"I thought you didn't like pie rhetoric," countered Markon, pushing aside the bed covers. He'd been better prepared last night: he'd worn a pair of loose trousers and one of his old fencing shirts to bed. Neither of them were particularly fine (the shirt in particular had more than a few darning scars, hence his mother's insistence upon shirts specifically for fencing) but they were loose and comfortable, and had the benefit of not creasing easily.

"I don't," said Althea, watching him tuck in the shirt and grope blindly for the light shoes he'd set aside. "It makes me hungry. I think I might have caught some of your Montalieran ways."

"Just as well," Markon said, carefully light-hearted. "If you're going to marry into the family you'd best start practising now."

Althea was difficult to see in the shadows, but Markon thought he caught a small, private, and entirely delightful smile as it flitted across her face. It was still in her voice as she said: "I had, hadn't I? Your shoes are over here."

They went through the back passages, following a thin, winding way through narrow halls and steep staircases that stirred in Markon's mind as vaguely familiar. It wasn't until Althea stopped at a meeting of corridors and counted three sconces from the left as they walked that he remembered why it was so familiar.

"Third to the left, warp and weft," he said. He reached past Althea and found the hidden catch in the sconce, which clicked beneath his fingertips and set off a dusty scraping of bricks in front of them.

"Oh," said Althea. She sounded disappointed. "How did you know which one it was?"

"I went searching for these passages when I was a boy," said Markon. "I never found this one, but Parrin did. It was one summer while he was recovering from a lingering chest infection. He was wrapped up in shawls and scarves, waddling around the castle with one of the younger upper maids and trying to find all the passages. He was so proud of himself for finding it. We made the rhyme so we'd remember."

"Warp and weft?" Althea said quizzically.

"Maker's mark," Markon told her. "This part of the castle was restored about thirty years ago after a bit of a nasty incident with a dragon– secret passage and all. The iron sconces were sourced from a local consortium of blacksmiths here in the capital known as The Metal Loom. All of their work was stamped with the sign of the Metal Loom."

"Now, that's interesting," said Althea thoughtfully.

"I asked them about it when Parrin found the passage and I recognised the maker's mark. They said the passage had been caved in before the dragon incident, filled with half a century's rubble, but my father had them clear it out and make it new. He was a great one for tradition, my father. Why do you suppose the Door was opened here? I didn't think anyone else knew about it."

"That's what so interesting," said Althea, and opened the Door.

The first impression Markon had was one of brilliant moonshine. It gleamed along marble flagstones and marble colonnades, sparkled in the depths of decorative pools, and glided gently on wafting leaves through the high arches of a foreign courtyard. The breeze was soft, intimate, and delicately scented.

"Unseelie," said Althea. "This bit of magic is particularly strong, so we can't count on an easy excursion this time."

Markon, who hadn't thought their last venture into Faery had gone particularly well, nodded and tried not to look as wary as he felt. "Is that music I hear?"

"Most likely," Althea said, drawing him through the Door and into Faery once again.

Markon stumbled slightly on the threshold, suspended for a brief moment between Here and There, and then the suspicion of music jumped in intensity as he found himself in the moonlit courtyard. It was a high, mad skirling of pipes and violins that tugged at his feet and made him smile instinctively. He looked at Althea and saw a gleam of sable in her eyes that suddenly made her seem fae again. Already she was floating rather than walking; and Markon, feeling that she might possibly float away into the wild revels he could hear through the colonnades, instinctively held onto her hand though they were safely through the Door.

"It must be a feast night," said Althea. She wafted over to the arches at the end of the courtyard, trailing Markon behind her. Much to Markon's surprise, the courtyard wasn't really a courtyard: it was more of a vast balcony, left open to the stars and overlooking another courtyard below. The lower courtyard was paved in black and white marble like the upper was, but only small, shifting bits of it could be seen through the whirling throng. The music was louder here, too: it felt as though it was making its way, living and wild, into his very blood.

"We're not fine enough to go down there," Althea said regretfully. "If I'd *known*...never mind, we'll just have to steal some clothes."

"*Steal* clothes?" Markon repeated numbly. He found himself being led by the hand back across the courtyard without being able to summon up the words to express how little he wanted to steal clothes from the fae.

With an air of reason, Althea said: "We'll give them back, of course."

"Of course!" echoed Markon. He let Althea drag him through another of the interminable arches and halfway down a silvery hall before it occurred to him to ask: "Where are we going to get clothes?"

"The laundry."

"Fae have laundries?"

"*Everybody* has a laundry," said Althea. "Even the fae. Someone has to do the washing, after all. And on a feast night there are bound to be some fae who've sent down multiple ensembles just in case they change their minds. They think it's amusing to create more work for the servants. Ah! This way!"

Half an hour later Althea had calmly breezed into the laundry to appropriate two matching ensembles and Markon had found them a suitably shadowed alcove in which to change. He went first, eschewing his comfortable trousers and loose-fitting fencing shirt for a carelessly laced and ridiculously fine black one, with matching black trousers that held a hint of moonlight in silver thread. While Althea changed he went in search of boots to match, his stockinged feet padding lightly against marble flagstones, and finally managed to pilfer a newly polished pair that were sitting outside one of the doors upstairs. They were slightly tight, but nothing a few hours of wear wouldn't stretch out.

When he returned to fetch Althea she was far from her usual tightly laced and upright self. Fortunately Markon saw her before she saw him. That gave him a chance to stifle the surprised hiss of breath that slipped from him and wipe the stunned expression from his face. Where Markon was wearing black threaded with silver, Althea had chosen to wear silver beaded with jet, darkly glinting in a soft and shimmering dress that caught every curve on its sweep to the ground. As alluring as that was, it was her unbraided hair that caught his gaze, falling in great, full curls well past her waist.

Markon took in another mesmerized breath through his teeth and went forward to meet her.

"*There* you are," said Althea when she saw him, her eyes bright and glad. "I thought you'd gotten lost."

"I had to go a bit further afield for the boots," Markon said, displaying them for her inspection.

"Very nice," Althea said approvingly. "We'd better get on, I think. The drums are getting faster, which means the stronger drink will soon be circulating."

Markon offered her his arm with alacrity: the thought of Althea in *that* dress among heavily drinking fae was not something he wanted to contemplate. Moreover, if he wasn't very much mistaken, both he and Althea were moving much more swiftly now as the music lightened their feet towards its source. It was an intoxicant in and of itself: it curled around them as they moved back across the upper courtyard and then became almost breathable as they descended the stairs toward the lower courtyard of shifting blue, black, and silver.

The babble of conversation and laughter rose around them, almost as loud as the music, and when Markon asked Althea: "Do you still have the trace?" he had to bend his head and almost shout it in her ear.

"Oh yes," said Althea in his ear, her voice clear and carrying. "I saw her as soon as we looked over the balcony before."

"If you knew who it was, why did we engage in this episode of dress-up?" demanded Markon, slightly annoyed.

"Because it's *her*," Althea said calmly, with a tiny jerk of her chin. "The Lady of the Revels."

The Lady of the Revels was a tall, graceful fae somewhere near the centre of the swirling throng, dancing swift and free amidst the laughing dancers, her silver hair flying. Some of the energy of the dance came directly from her, Markon was sure: it seemed to coil around her and whorl outward, sparking a wild circle all around her that was clear to him despite the fact that he was no magic practitioner. On the face of it, it seemed as though it should be very easy to get to her: she was alone and vulnerable in the centre of the dance. But that was only, thought Markon, used to looking for guards in a crowd, if you didn't happen to notice the three *very* large fae who were part of the inner circle but also danced alone. Or the dozen that dotted the crowd all around, their eyes constantly moving, shifting and slipping through the dancers around them. Or even, he realised, his eyes slipping further afield, the slender young fae who was ostensibly drunk and well supplied with edible goodies, sitting in a tree just out of the dancers. That was certainly a quiver tucked behind him in the boughs—Markon could see the fletching of the arrows against the moonlight—and he was almost certain that he could see the curve of the bow as it blended in with the other branches.

"We wouldn't get as far as the inner circle before her guards stopped us," Althea said, unconsciously echoing Markon's thoughts. "This way, at least we look the part. And if we play our cards right, *she'll* come to *us*."

"Which way is the right way to play our cards?"

"She's female," said Althea. Unnecessarily, as he thought, until she added: "Fae women are good leaders, but they have their weak points. For instance, in a Fae Lady's court, whether Unseelie or Seelie, the unconscious bias will always be against men and for women."

"For example?" prompted Markon, aware that Althea was leading up to an already decided plan.

"For example," said Althea, giving him a prim, approving smile; "If a Fae Lady were to see a boorish human—or even a boorish fae—trying to foist his attentions upon a fae woman, she would intervene immediately and most likely personally."

"Most likely?"

"There's a chance she could order her archer over there to shoot you instead," said Althea. "But only a very slight one, and if we move out of his eye-line you'll be safe. She's powerful enough to feel confident intervening by herself."

"What do you mean by *foisting attentions*, exactly?" asked Markon, with deep foreboding.

"You'll have to pretend to back me up against something and try to kiss me."

"Oh." There didn't seem to be much to say to that, apart from: "What do you mean, try?"

"I'll be resisting, of course," said Althea.

"But—"

"I won't slap you *very* hard," she promised.

"*Althea*," said Markon, somewhat exasperatedly. Heavens knew it wasn't that he didn't want to kiss her. The problem was that he *did*, and he was certain that he shouldn't.

"It's either that or you'll have to pretend to be about to drive a dagger into me," pointed out Althea. "It's far harder to play that convincingly, and if you did it's far more likely she'd send her guards to deal with you. You've– *oh!*"

Markon had the pleasure of seeing her for once utterly surprised, blue eyes wide and startled as he pinned her arms to her sides and kissed her. She put up an impressive struggle, but Markon had the advantage and it wasn't until he let her go that she could slap him. He thought he might have been grinning when her palm connected with his cheek, and though he gasped he wasn't sure it quite did away with the smile in his eyes.

"I believe the lady is requesting your absence," said a cold, silvery voice at his ear. Markon jerked away from the sound much as he would have torn himself away from a poisonous snake, and the Lady twined herself around him until she was between him and Althea, the edge of one cool, pale cheek toward him and her gaze resting on Althea. "Are you well, little one?" she asked.

"Yes," said Althea, but her voice was slightly breathless, which pleased Markon greatly. He couldn't see her for the Lady's willowy, black-edged form, but what he had seen before she intervened was a deep, warm flush in Althea's cheeks. "Thank you for your assistance, Lady."

The Lady's eyes flicked from Althea and back to Markon. She said: "Perhaps I've mistaken the situation. Do you require my assistance, little one?"

"No," said Althea, bringing one hand out from the folds of her borrowed skirt. "I believe you need mine."

Again there was a flicking of the Lady's eyes from one to the other. "We will speak privately," she said.

They were courteously escorted to what Markon thought might have been the Lady's private quarters: an enormous suite of rooms that numbered among them a pleasant, leafy apartment with grass for carpet and a waterfall leaping from the ceiling in one corner. It was to this leafy space that they were escorted, and though their escort was perfectly polite and well-mannered,

Markon had the distinct impression that if either he or Althea took one step outside the prescribed course, they would be stabbed through the heart without a word or a second thought.

For all their solicitude, when the guards had walked them to the door they left them alone with the Lady. It should have made Markon feel more comfortable, but instead it made him feel disagreeably that the Lady didn't consider them to be a significant threat– and worse, that they just might *not* be. Althea had said that this magic was much stronger than the first lot they'd trailed, and he remembered too that she'd said this wouldn't be an easy trip like that one had been.

Still, when the Lady closed the door on them she seemed perfectly cool: relaxed even. Markon wondered if he'd imagined the momentary freezing of her face when she'd seen what Althea held.

Her voice as languorous as her eyes were watchful, the Lady said: "How did you happen to come by that little bauble?"

"Bauble?" said Althea seriously. "No. I don't think so. I think this *little bauble* cost you rather a lot."

"In bitter pride and anger, quite significantly," agreed the Lady. "What do you know, little one?"

"I know there was a Door drawn and open. I know you were in the human world and that you laid at least one spell while you were there."

"And you wish to know more?"

"I do," said Althea.

"Something to do with your strong, silent human, hm?"

"It concerns my son," said Markon.

"You: silence," said the Lady, utterly indifferent. "I care nothing for humans and their get, nor do I appreciate being a pawn in the games of your snivelling kind. That I should be summoned like a common demon and forced to do the bidding of a puny, magicless stripling! *I*, who rule three cantons in the Unseelie! And to know that it could happen again!"

"If you answer our questions we'll do our best to make sure it doesn't happen again," said Althea, a warning in her eyes for Markon. "That's why we're here. There's a rogue human opening Doors to Faery and harming young ladies in the court. Yesterday we met an old fae who said she was paying a debt to the Opener."

"Debt!" said the Lady scornfully. "Oh well, I suppose in the strictest sense of things she was telling the truth. The spell laid a burden on me that I couldn't shake off: it felt for all the world that I'd struck a bargain and entered into a debt of honour. I dispensed with some of my ire on the human girl whose bones I shattered, but I would fain see that human stripling again!"

"Would you know the human again?"

The lady laughed derisively. "One human is much the same as another, and the knave wore a hooded cloak. I couldn't so much as tell whether it was male or female. The spell, though: I'd know it again. One thing is certain, little one: *that* spell was not such as belonged with *that* human."

"I see," said Althea thoughtfully.

"I went away without seeking vengeance this time," said the Lady, and there was a chill in her voice that cut right to Markon's bones. "Next time I will not be so lenient."

"Lenient!" he said, with a slow-burning anger that overtook the chill from the Lady's voice. "Lenient! The child's bones were shattered so that they couldn't be healed before they began to shatter again!"

"Oh, I can see why you keep him!" purred the Lady. "Such passion! And yet, my little one, if your human does not mind his manners I'll not find it necessary to mind *mine*."

"Be silent," Althea tossed at Markon, offhand and imperious. He shut his mouth, his anger enough in check to read the tension in her shoulders.

The Lady smiled at his acquiescence and turned her gaze on Althea again. "I would fain have my magic back, little one."

"It's yours," said Althea, shaking out her hand as if to rid it of a gaudy bracelet no longer in favour. "Do you have any other recollections that may be of help to us?"

"Only one," said the Lady, and Markon very much misliked the cruel curve of her lips. "The magic you carry will bring you nothing but trouble if you travel overlong in Faery. Be cautious, little one, and good fortune!"

# 7

## DAY SEVEN

It was an odd way to put it, thought Markon. Yesterday in Faery the Lady of the Revels had said: *The magic you carry will bring you nothing but trouble.* Not *your magic*, but *the magic you carry*. And although Althea gave a very good impression of being fae, Markon had the feeling that it wasn't so easy to hoodwink the Lady of the Revels. He did try to find out from Althea exactly what the fae had meant, but Althea had been distant and uncommunicative on the way back to the castle. Whether that was because she was hiding something or because she was unsettled from the kiss, Markon wasn't quite sure.

He found himself smiling absently at the window and hastily pushed away that particular memory. Far too many of his thoughts revolved around Althea as it was: there was no need to encourage dangerous and ultimately ineligible thoughts. Althea belonged to Parrin.

He therefore did *not* think about her as he finished the final draft of the Montalier/Avernse trade agreement. He didn't think about her in her moonlight dress with her hair curling down her back. He didn't think about her strawberry shortcake scent or her bouncing, energetic walk. He didn't think about her single-minded determination or her habit of forgetting that she was talking to the Reigning Monarch of Montalier. He was so intent upon not thinking about Althea, in fact, that when she and Parrin entered the library together, he wasn't entirely sure that he hadn't conjured her up.

"What mischief are you up to?"

They both had a troubled look, and before Parrin answered, they exchanged a look.

"Doctor Romalier is dead."

Markon's first thought was one of galling frustration that even dead, Doctor Romalier was going to cause him immense annoyance. A Wyndsor doctor, dead on Montalieran soil: what Wyndsor *couldn't* do with this as their incitement!

"What happened?"

"I'm not entirely sure," said Althea. "He's in his room, throat cut, but there isn't a lot of blood."

"There was heaps," said Parrin, who looked slightly green.

"Not enough," Althea said firmly. "When you cut someone's throat—"

"*Althea!*" groaned Parrin. "You told me before, and it was just as awful then! You're trying to make me throw up again."

"You took Parrin to see the body?" demanded Markon.

"Of course!" said Althea, evidently surprised. "He was with me, and it's his affair, too. Besides, I couldn't find you."

"I've been in the library all morning," Markon said, and caught the way her eyes slid past him. Oho! So it *was* the kiss!

"When you cut someone's throat," she reiterated; "There is spatter. And spurting. And huge puddles of blood."

Parrin grew slightly greener. "Althea—"

"And there was none of that," continued Althea, ignoring him.

"Perhaps someone used magic on him," Markon suggested. Plain, personal murder was in short supply at the moment. It would be almost refreshing to know that someone had merely slit the doctor's throat.

"No magic at all," said Althea. "It had me at a bit of a loss, actually. I'm so prepared for your murders to be magical ones that it took me quite a while to understand that his throat really was slit."

"They're not *my* murders," Markon protested.

"But the point I was trying to make," continued Althea, with a disapproving look at Parrin: "Was that he wasn't killed in his room. Someone killed him elsewhere and then moved the body."

Markon frowned. "Why?"

"I suppose he was killed somewhere that would implicate the murderer," said Althea. "And that really does make me wonder if perhaps we're looking for a man. Throat-slitting is such a messy way of killing someone."

"It doesn't need much strength, though," pointed out Markon.

Althea looked dissatisfied. "Yes. I suppose you'll be quite busy this afternoon contacting Wyndsor and making official statements?"

"Yes," said Markon, rather sourly. "Which begs the question of why I've not seen my seneschal yet."

"I'm sure he'll come just as soon as he knows."

Markon narrowed his eyes first at Althea, then Parrin. "And when *will* he know?"

"Possibly when the upper maid who discovered Doctor Romalier regains consciousness," said Althea. "I think her name is Nan. She must have come to draw his curtains."

"Did you leave the poor girl on the floor?"

"I thought it would be easier than explaining why we were prying into Doctor Romalier's room," Althea said, a little guiltily. "Besides, it gave us a chance to come and tell you."

"If it comes to that, why were you prying into Doctor Romalier's room?" asked Markon. "For that matter, how did you get in?"

"Althea can pick locks," said Parrin, radiating awe. "She said she'll teach me how to do it."

Althea's eyes met Markon's. She said hastily: "I said I *might* teach you. We wanted to see if there was anything interesting in Doctor Romalier's rooms. After that listening spell he was certain would be in my suite, I thought a little poking around in *his* suite might prove helpful."

"Only we didn't get a chance to look because Doctor Romalier was dead on the floor and the maid was unconscious by the door," said Parrin.

"Really?" Markon found himself surprised. Althea's eagerness for investigation hadn't been stopped by a mere dead body last time.

"Well, I might have pinched some of Doctor Romalier's notes," confessed Althea. "As galling as it is to think, he must have been very close to discovering who's opening the doors: why kill him otherwise? I thought the notes might be enlightening. We didn't dare stay too long in case the maid came around. Besides, Parrin was just about to throw up."

"And were the notes helpful?"

"Not particularly," said Althea. "Doctor Romalier was working under the theory that these attacks were—*ahem*—'spiteful womanish crimes' and that it was likely they were committed by one of the female servants in the lower castle."

"Why the servants in the lower castle?" asked Markon wearily, certain that he was about to be sorry that he'd asked.

"Apparently 'the lower class are prone to envying their betters'," said Althea distastefully. "Oh dear, I think this must be your seneschal coming now. Perhaps I'll go and talk to Nan."

Markon would have protested that he wanted to come along as well, but it would have sounded perilously like whining. If it *was* his seneschal he would be far too busy being Informed and writing tiresome letters to Wyndsor to sneak about the castle with Althea. And now that he came to think of Wyndsor, thought Markon bleakly, he was bound to have to talk to Pilburn again. Doctor Romalier and the emissary had both been irritating and potentially dangerous thorns in his side, but the murder of either of them in his castle was more than slightly embarrassing. And if he wasn't careful, it could also be more than slightly damaging.

The best thing, thought Markon, nodding a distracted goodbye to Althea and Parrin as they slipped from the library, would be to let it get about that Doctor Romalier had fallen a victim to the curse. After all, he'd been sent from Wyndsor—that all-too-interested and solicitous country—specifically for the purpose of assisting with the curse. It was by no means certain that he *hadn't* been murdered in pursuance of breaking the curse.

Althea and Parrin were scarcely gone when there was a knock at the library door; firm, business-like, and short. That settled it: it must be his seneschal. No one else could make a simple knock at the door sound both authorative and vaguely menacing.

"Enter!" he called.

The door opened and closed with precise movements; and having entered the room, Markon's seneschal bowed in equally precise movements.

"Good afternoon, Sal."

"Sire."

"I suppose you've come to tell me about Doctor Romalier's murder?"

His seneschal's face became slightly more granite than usual. "Is this something I should not know about, sire?"

"I don't see why," said Markon. "If I'm to be annoyed by it you may as well be annoyed, too."

A grin broke out across Sal's usually impassive face. "I'm glad to hear it, sire. You had me worried. I'm no lover of hush work."

"Not hush work," Markon said, sighing faintly. "But it may well be tricky."

"If you don't mind my asking, sire: if it's not hush work, how did you know?"

"The enchantress and Doctor Romalier were both working on the curse."

"Ay, a rarely knowing woman, that one," said Sal approvingly. "Found the body, did she?"

"She did. Perhaps you could be careful about where you mention the fact."

"Ay, sire. You're certain she didn't do it?"

"I am. She had Parrin with her at the time."

His seneschal nodded. "Good fortune, that. One of the upper maids found the body first and brought in the steward. He brought her to me, of course. She was in a bit of a state: couldn't say anything but that he'd been murdered just like her best friend, and that it wouldn't stop until they were all dead. I had to have her looked after by one of the nurses."

"Her best friend murdered, too?"

"Ay, sire. Happens that the young girl murdered four nights ago was her dear friend. They worked together and were by all accounts very close. I'm told that Nan took prodigious care of the girl: they quilted rugs together in their spare time and gossiped about the other upper maids."

"Poor child," said Markon. "Unfortunate that she was the one to find the doctor."

"Do you have instructions for me?"

"Not many. I'm about to start on the express to Wyndsor, so I'll need your preliminary report before dinner. And I'd appreciate it if you sent the Wyndsor Emissary in to me: he'll need to be told."

"I could go so far as to tell him myself, sire," suggested Sal. "No need for you to be bothered, I dare say."

It was very tempting. Markon would much rather not converse with Pilburn if he didn't have to do so. At last, he shook his head ruefully and said: "On the whole, I think not. I wouldn't like Wyndsor to feel itself slighted, and if there's anything Pilburn is adroit at doing, it's taking offense. Send him up to me when you're able."

"As you say sire," said Sal, bowing once again. "I'll have the report to you in time for the night express."

That night before bed Markon slipped an etched iron band onto each of his wrists. He'd become rather tired of relying upon Althea for his protection while in Faery, and after some frustrated thought on the matter it had seemed likely that his armoury would have something helpful in it.

It did: a pair of etched iron bands that were locked away in a beautiful rowan-wood box bearing a card with the somewhat gloomy message:

Markel,

*To you and your bride I give this gift in the hope that you may never need to use it. Knowing something of this world and **that**, and knowing something of the Broken Sword itself, I feel certain that those who are prepared will better weather the storm I foresee drawing near. Should I live to see you bear children, I will do them the same kindness.*

Yours in hope,

*Simel*

Markon, having seen Faery for himself, had a good idea of what *that world* was; and he distantly remembered that his father had once had an older brother, Simel. No one would talk of him, but the impression that had grown in the young Markon from things that *were* said was of a deeply troubled and perhaps slightly mad man. Still, when Markon showed the iron bands to Doctor Fenke, the man stared at him and asked forthrightly: "What would your majesty be needing with Dispelling Bands?"

"I'm not sure I do need them," said Markon. "I'm rather curious to know what they are, however. I found them in my father's things."

"They protect the wearer against malicious Faery magic," said Doctor Fenke, his suspicions not entirely allayed. He'd gone on to say a great deal more, but Markon had already come to the conclusion that it would behove him well to wear them on the next excursion into Faery. Perhaps tomorrow he would ask Althea about them.

# 8

## DAY EIGHT

"Unseelie again," said Markon, peering into the soft darkness of the Door. "I'm beginning to sense a pattern."

"There's not too much difference between Seelie and Unseelie when it comes to humans," Althea said matter-of-factly. "To them we're more like talking dogs than anything. The Seelie are just as happy to murder us as the Unseelie: the only difference is that they'll do it with a smile instead of a wink."

"I see," said Markon, grateful for the twin iron bands around his wrists. "Speaking of murder, which particular bit of magic do we have to thank for bringing us to this piece of Faery?"

"Sal was showing me some of the sights yesterday afternoon," said Althea. "I found a few remnants of magic where Parrin's first sweetheart and one of the women who tried to break the curse were last seen. It's– well, it seems familiar, but I can't place it."

"Does the room look familiar?"

"I can't even tell it *is* a room," said Althea, reaching for Markon's hand. "Familiar or otherwise. Are you ready?"

Markon wrapped his fingers tightly around Althea hand, said: "Oh, about as much as usual," and stepped through the Door with her. At first there was only confusion and soft darkness, while they stood hand in hand to get their bearings.

Then a male voice said: "What a delicious surprise!" from somewhere in the velvet darkness. It was soft, smooth, and entirely seductive.

Althea said: "Bother!"

"Sweetness, that's not very kind of you," said the voice reproachfully.

Markon, his teeth set on edge, flexed the fingers of his free hand in an instinctive desire to wrap them around the throat of the speaker. He couldn't make out anything in the darkness, but as he frowned into the shadows a flare of silver burst into being and swiftly formed a swirling ball that lit the entire room. In its light, a rather annoyed Althea could be seen, her gaze directed toward the rumpled bed where a half-naked male fae was lounging. He yawned and stretched sinuously for Althea's benefit, then rolled lightly across the wine-coloured bedspread and to his feet.

"I thought I recognised the magic," said Althea. "I should have picked another sample."

"You cut me to the quick," sighed the fae. His eyes flicked over her in a way that immediately doubled Markon's desire strangle him, but it wasn't until the fae strolled over and curled one arm around Althea's waist that he said curtly: "I take it you know each other?"

"Oh yes," said the fae, lowering his head in what Markon had no doubt was an attempt to kiss her.

Althea, putting one hand on his bare chest to push him away firmly, said: "Not particularly. Carmine, if you try to kiss me again, I'll–"

Through his teeth, Markon said: "Again?"

"Sweetness, the company you keep is slipping decidedly," said Carmine. He released Althea but still stood by far too close.

"This isn't a social call!" said Althea. She sounded harried. "Markon, this is Carmine. He tried to buy me some years ago.

Carmine, this is Markon. He's my human, and if you even think about–"

"I'm not your human," said Markon grimly.

Carmine said: "I wanted to marry you, sweetness. There's a difference."

Althea looked rather helplessly from Markon to Carmine; and Markon, in spite of his annoyance, began to grin. "We're here for information," he told the fae. "You saw us come through the Door, I take it? Well, fae are being pulled through to the human world and forced to attack human women."

"Believe me, I know," said Carmine, his teeth showing in a half-snarl. "And could I catch the little wench, I'd show her a thing or two!"

Markon's eyes snapped to the fae's face. "Wench? It was a woman?"

At the same time, Althea said: "Are you *sure*?"

"My darling sweetness, I trust I may know a female figure through something so flimsy as a cloak, no matter *how* well her face is hid. What's more, she was playing with a spell not of her own making."

"So we were led to believe," said Althea. "You were called through more than once, weren't you? I found pieces of your magic where at least two of the girls disappeared."

"You know my kind heart," said Carmine, winking at her. "The burden was to kill, injure, or steal. I chose to steal: to damage a human maiden was more than I could bear."

"Well, you've got to give them back now," said Althea. Markon was unpleasantly aware that she wasn't keeping up the act of being fae with this particular fae. Apparently she didn't feel the need to pretend with him.

"I've always loved your optimism, my sweetness," said Carmine, sliding his arm around her waist again to pull her close. He looked down at her through his eyelashes and murmured: "Whatever makes you think I'll give up my new subjects to you?"

Althea said: "I wish you'd put on a shirt, Carmine. You know you can't win me over with your tricks, and I honestly don't know why you still try."

"I hold a cherished hope that one day they might work," said Carmine, with a crooked smile; but he let her go and threw himself on the bed again. "The older lady you may not have. She's sworn fealty to me and I'd be sorry to lose her. The younger you may have in exchange for a certain promise."

Althea narrowed her eyes at him. "*What* promise?"

"Certainly not any that you're thinking of," Carmine said piously. "For shame! Perhaps I'd give her up freely if I could, but as it happens I am not free to give her up under the burden laid on me. But if I were to have another burden laid on me—a bargain struck that named her as payment of my side of the bargain—well, who knows what bargains humans will make, after all?"

"What is it you want?" asked Markon. He, like Althea, was highly suspicious of the fae's motives.

"I'm glad you asked that, human," said Carmine affably. "There's a certain curio owned by a...ah, friend...of mine. He's decidedly set on keeping it, too, the cur!"

"Fancy that," said Althea. "I suppose you want us to steal it."

"The thought did cross my mind, sweetness. You've such a talent for it, after all."

"Contract, or handshake?" asked Althea, and to Markon's mind it looked as though she was blushing faintly.

"Oh, a handshake between friends, of course," said Carmine; and then, more formally: "I will turn the girl over to you."

"We will steal your curio," said Althea, as formally. She shook the hand that Carmine offered, a quick, precise gesture. "Where is it?"

"Why don't we sit down with something to drink," said Carmine, his teeth gleaming silver. "This could take a little time to explain. I'm so glad you called, sweetness! And to think that I was bored today!"

"How are we going to get in there?" said Markon despairingly, some time later. In front of them rose a mountain as glossy as it was steep, entirely made of glass. "It's glass! It's a mountain of glass!"

"It is, isn't it?" said Althea. Her blue eyes were dark with amusement, her cheeks whipped pink from the snowy breeze that tugged at her braid. "I'd forgotten how lovely it looks under the full moon. They do love their beautiful, impossibly geography, the Unseelie."

"I suppose that explains the snow as well."

"No, it usually snows around here," said Althea. "It's at a higher altitude than the rest of the cantons. Whenever I came here–"

She stopped. Markon, who was conscious of a grinding jealousy, said in a carefully colourless voice: "You spent a lot of time here, I gather?"

"The only happy moments I had in Faery were spent here," Althea said. "I was generally kept in a much more...oppressive...atmosphere."

"He made your life happier?"

Althea laughed. "He made it more interesting. There's always a game afoot with Carmine."

"So I see," said Markon, with a significant look at the glass mountain that rose before them, high and sparkling in the moonlight. "I wonder what he wants with this sword."

"Shard," Althea corrected absently. "And so do I. A broken sword isn't generally held to be a useful thing. Even as a magical artefact a single shard of it doesn't seem likely to be particularly helpful."

"More importantly, how are we supposed to get *in* there? It's a pity Carmine couldn't tell us more."

"I've got a few ideas about that," said Althea.

"I thought you might," Markon murmured. "Do any of them involve me kissing you?"

There was a brief pause before Althea said: "Not this time."

"What a shame," said Markon, enjoying himself all the more when he saw the deepening of colour in her cheeks.

Althea put her chin up slightly and said: "In the legends it's all eagles and apples, but that's to climb the mountain."

"And we want to get *in*," he agreed, allowing the refocus of subject.

"On the other hand, what the knights and princes wanted was on top of the mountain in the stories."

"Yes, but those are only stories, aren't they?"

"Stories in Faery are never just stories," Althea said seriously, kicking up tiny flurries of snow as she started energetically toward the mountain.

Markon belatedly started after her, kicking up his own miniature snow-storms. "What do eagles and apples have to do with it all?"

"Something to do with an apple tree that produces golden apples, growing on the top of the glass mountain."

"It seems unlikely," said Markon. "But I suppose if we're not sniffing at a tree that grows golden apples we can't be too worried about how it grows on a mountain of glass, after all. I suppose the apples were greatly sought after."

"Oh yes," said Althea, placing one hand on the great glass base of the mountain. "If a man could get a golden apple from the top of the glass mountain and bring it to the king of the canton, he'd give the man his daughter in marriage."

"I wonder what he wanted with the apple," said Markon curiously. "A bride-price for a princess is worth a lot more than a golden apple, no matter how odd it may be."

"It makes you wonder what was wrong with the princess," nodded Althea. "But there were a lot of suitors regardless: including, in the end, a young schoolboy who cut the paws off a lynx and clawed halfway up the glass mountain. The eagle, which was there to fight off all comers, thought he was carrion and swooped for him. The schoolboy seized it by the feet and held on tightly even when the eagle rose in the air to shake him off, and the eagle carried him the rest of the way to the top of the mountain."

Markon, who was staring at her in patent amazement, said: "That poor princess! Did she have to marry the schoolboy, I wonder?"

"More than likely," said Althea absently. She was studying the glass monstrosity with a frown. "The fae are horribly fair when it comes to honouring promises. There has to be a door here somewhere."

"Maybe we can find a handy lynx to slaughter," said Markon, grinning.

"Claws!" said Althea. "Of course! Well, why not?"

"Why not indeed?" Markon said, completely out of his depth.

Althea tipped her head at a section of mountain slightly to their right, and he saw what she meant. There were parallel scorings in the glass that ran from just under shoulder height to the snow: two sets of them. If he looked at them the right way, he could almost imagine that they *were* claw marks. If a lynx's claws were capable of scoring glass, that is.

"No lintel, though."

"I don't expect we'll have to actually *kill* a lynx," said Althea doubtfully. "See if your nails can make a cross-section, Markon. Fingers *and* thumb, I think."

"Your nails are longer," said Markon, but he did as he was told. There was a painful shriek of nails against glass, and when he pulled his hand away a fresh set of scratches marred the glass from one set of vertical scratches to the other.

"Yes," Althea said; "But I have a feeling that the mountain likes to challenge men particularly."

Markon put his palms flat against the rectangle of glass and pushed. Much to his satisfaction, it sank inward with barely a sliver of sound, and disappeared into the dark blue interior of the glass mountain. "I think you may be right," he said. He was deeply reluctant to venture into that yawning rectangle of dark blue shadow, but Althea was already ducking beneath his nail-marked lintel and into the mountain, and he found that he was even more reluctant to let her out of his sight. Markon followed her into the mountain.

The passage was at first quite rough, with dull cuttings of glass crunching ominously beneath their feet, but before long it grew sleeker and wider, and they began to see the smooth edges where it joined another passage up ahead. Behind them, Markon heard the glass doorway snick back into place and closed his eyes briefly in resignation. He could only hope that they would be able to get back out when the time came.

Althea, who had eagerly pressed ahead, called to him from the joining of the passages. "Come and see, Markon!"

He did, and found that the passage theirs joined had a small cutting that gave access to a view of what was to come. He was entirely unsurprised to note that they were looking down on a crawling, sprawling mess of glass walls, ways, and tunnels.

"What a warren!" he said, with a sigh.

"Not a warren!" Althea said, her eyes sparkling: "A maze! I wonder why Carmine didn't tell us."

"I suppose it's possible that Carmine doesn't know quite everything," Markon said dryly. Carmine, he privately considered, hadn't known anything *like* enough about this venture.

"Left or right?"

"Eagles," said Markon, and pointed at the glass corner to his left. His eyes met Althea's, as bright as hers were, and then flicked back to the tiny etching of an eagle that decorated it.

Althea clapped her hands. "Wonderful! How clever of you to– *oh!–*"

Markon, who hadn't quite caught the soft *swoosh* of something glassy as it slipped through the blue shadows, saw a flower of dark red blossom on the shoulder of Althea's green dress and flung both himself and her around the corner before the second sliver shattered against the wall.

"Oh!" said Althea again, panting. "That hurts...rather a lot, actually. What was that?"

"Hold still," said Markon, his fingers digging into her shoulder. The shaft of glass still protruded from her shoulder, needle thin and horribly delicate. He drew it from her flesh little by little, slick with blood, while Althea gripped her lip with her teeth and tried to breath very carefully, then cast it aside to shatter on the floor and pulled aside the shoulder of her gown with bloody fingers.

"I didn't see it coming," Althea said, pressing a hand to the open wound in spite of Markon's ministrations. "It's only a small hole, Markon."

"Small, but deep and bleeding freely," Markon said grimly. "We'd best keep moving, I think."

Althea conjured a small, flowing ribbon of light to ripple along the passage floor in front of them, pushing back the shadows briefly. As reassurance went it was a double-edged sword: it certainly made their way easier to see in the cold blue light, but the flickering shadows it formed had Markon's eyes darting at every fluctuation.

"Did you see where the glass shard came from?" asked Althea. Her eyes were also searching the shadows, and the patch of blood on her shoulder was rapidly spreading.

"No. Whatever it was, it was behind us."

"I know," said Althea. "But there was only the door behind us."

"Is there anything about glass shards in the stories?"

"Not a word. Oh. Markon, look to the left."

To their left was a dead end. The rippling light of Althea's magical ambiance played on the wall; which, at a variance to all the other walls around them, was oddly lumpy. Markon tried to tell himself that the lumps only seemed to bulge and grow because of the shifting of the light, but when the suggestion of a head and torso thrust themselves free from the wall, quickly followed by a second glass head and torso, it was impossible to lie to himself any longer.

"We should walk a little faster," said Althea decidedly, but Markon was already hurrying her away from the dead end.

"Do you think it was one of them that did it?"

"They're the only other things that are moving in here," Althea said. "Bother! There are more of them!"

Markon, who had already seen them—had seen, moreover, the ominous way in which two spike-laden appendages were brought to bear on himself and Althea—seized Althea around the waist and whirled them both down the next passage, regardless of its inscription. Shards of glass spat and splintered at the corner, stinging the back of his neck and biting into his side. Althea, caught close to his chest and shielded from the worst of it by Markon's body, said in his ear: "Was it an eagle?"

"Don't know," Markon said tersely. "Keep going: they're following."

"I'll lead," Althea said, snatching at his hand. "You watch for the glass men."

It could have been a nightmare, Markon thought, except for the warmth of Althea's fingers. They left a trail of blood drops that would have distracted him if he hadn't been so focused on watching out for more of the glass men. Althea guided him through it, quietly frustrated whenever Markon swept her implacably down the wrong passage to escape another pair of glass men, and unable to use her ripple of light to read inscriptions for fear of drawing more of them. Fortunately the tangle of passages and covered walkways seemed to be more of a puzzle than a maze, and for every wrong way that they were forced to take Althea managed to get them back on the right track like a small, perfectly poised hound.

As they ran, blood trickled down Markon's collar from the cuts on the back of his neck. It occurred to him that there was more blood than there should be, and when he looked down at Althea in the dark blue light of a covered walkway, he thought she was paler than she had been, the whole left side of her bodice stained dark red.

"Althea?"

"It's fine," she said, with something of a gasp. "I'll see if I can heal it once we have a moment to rest. Now that we're not lighting up the walkways or making too much noise we should be able to sneak about the passages more easily. Do you have a handkerchief?"

Markon did. He pulled the ironed and scented square from his pocket, annoyed at himself for not having thought of it himself, and hastily tied it around Althea's shoulder and under her arm.

"Make it tight," she said, chafing her left hand with her right. And then, in a rather different voice: "Did any of the spikes hit you? You're bleeding."

"Only splinters," Markon said, tugging his knot tight. "They shattered on the wall. Why?"

"Never mind," said Althea, curling her left hand into her skirts. "I'll fix that when we get out, too. Let's keep going."

They crept through the passages like blue ghosts themselves, stealing past rapidly forming glass men and dashing through intersections that held men from earlier skirmishes. It seemed that once the glass men formed and separated from the walls, they remained in the passages.

They were both panting by the time they stumbled into a high, arched rotunda from which myriad passages spiralled into the navy darkness.

"Found it!" said Althea, her laugh low and weary. Markon put his arm around her waist, staining his own shirt with blood, and drew her toward the low, glassy table that stood in the centre of the rotunda. On it was a small glass case with a small glass door that was shut by a complicated glasswork mechanism. Inside the glass case, innocuous and slightly dirty, was a sizeable shard of metal that looked like it had once been part of a great broadsword.

"What is it?" asked Markon, his breath fogging the glass. "You can't tell me he wants a simple scrap from an old sword."

Althea hung over the display, her hand gripping a fistful of Markon's shirt for support. "I don't know. It's horribly powerful, but it's benevolent– and oh! it's connected to so many things! But it's...*shielded* from me. Why would it be shielded from me? It's human-made..."

Althea's voice trailed away, and Markon heard her say a soft, sorrowful: "Oh."

"What is it?"

"It's nothing," said Althea, but there was a pinch of sorrow to the corners of her eyes. "We can't leave this with Carmine. It's not the sort of thing that should be in Faery."

Markon threw a wary look around at the passages that surrounded them. "We should take it and keep going. Will it attract *them* when we open the case?"

"Probably," Althea said, and opened the case. She snatched the shard from its bed of velvet and said to him: "We'd better start running now. It set off every magical alarm in the mountain."

Markon grabbed her by the hand with an exasperated look, but when he tried to pull her back the way they'd come, she said swiftly: "Not eagles this time! Apples!" and dragged him toward one of the other passages instead.

"Why are we going back by a different way?" he said, catching sight of the tiny trio of apples that was carved into the wall.

"Because it's claws, then eagles, *then* apples!" said Althea. "*Duck*, Markon!"

Three glass spikes zipped over his head and shattered at the end of the passage. Markon, bent almost double and close to stumbling, hauled Althea around the next corner and headlong into four of the glass men.

"No!" said Althea, in a small, panting voice. Markon ruthlessly seized her despite her struggles, wrapping his arms around her and turning his back to the men. Then he ran, lifting her bodily from the ground, her head shielded in his shoulder, bypassing the intersection from which they'd come.

He didn't even feel the spikes when they entered his flesh. He knew they were there, because as he ran with Althea clasped tightly to his chest and the shard of the sword between them, blunt and heavy, he saw them in the wall reflections that flanked him. "Apples," he said, when his heavy legs felt like they couldn't go any faster. "Apples and then we're out." And he hoped with all his heart that it was so.

Markon would never remember exactly how he got out of the glass mountain. There were myriad etchings of apples and even more appearances of the glass men, who despite the lack of Althea's magic light, seemed to hone in on them with deadly accuracy. He ran further than it seemed possible for them to have journeyed already, and at last he was running in snow, under the ridiculously beautiful Faery sky with its high, full moon.

He put Althea down rather less gently than he'd meant to, feeling a stiffness in his arms that was far from natural. She gave a little sob, the shard dropping to the snow, and Markon opened his mouth to apologise but found that it, too, was stiff.

"Sit down," said Althea shakily, one hand bearing him down into the snow. The pinky and middle fingers of that hand were hard and glossy and...glasslike. Markon tried to tell her so but his mouth wouldn't move. Neither did the snow feel cold beneath him, and the cuts on his neck no longer hurt. In fact, nothing seemed to hurt.

And then Althea began to remove the glass spikes one by one: ten or so of them. That *did* hurt, a hopeful, agonising promise that perhaps he could be stopped from turning to glass after all. She worked quickly, drawing and discarding in one motion, but it was a long time after she finished drawing out the spikes that Markon became aware that he could feel her hands on his back, and that he could move again. He turned to pull Althea into his lap despite the aching of his muscles, holding her close in relief that she was still there, still alive, still flesh. Althea suffered it for a moment that was far too short, then disengaged herself and set snow flurrying as she rose.

Markon also climbed stiffly to his feet, while Althea picked up the shard again and slipped it into her pocket. She said: "Is that better?"

He flexed his shoulders, relieved to find that the muscles stretched and bowed as they normally did.

"Yes," he said. "That is– yes, I think so."

Althea boxed his ears. It was quick, violent, and entirely unexpected; and it sprawled him back into the snow from which he'd risen.

Entirely shocked, Markon said: "What?"

"I was already poisoned," Althea said. The words came out slowly, and it was borne in on him that she was so angry that she was finding it hard to speak. "I was holding it back enough to last. A few more spikes wouldn't have stopped that. *Don't ever do that again.*"

"I was protecting you!" said Markon, scrambling to his feet once more.

"I know," snapped Althea. "Don't do it again!" She hugged him fiercely, bloodying the front of his shirt as well, but before Markon could respond in kind she pushed him away and turned her back on him to ascend the hill. Markon stared after her straight, angry spine for a perplexed moment, then hurried after her.

"I'm not going to stop protecting you," he told her severe profile, when he caught up with her.

Then, because she was as white and weary as death, he put his arm around her waist again. When he felt her arm go around his waist again, gripping a handful of shirt as it had done in the glass mountain, he couldn't help the smile that spread over his face.

"What's this, sweetness?"

Carmine's voice was light, but Markon saw the swift step forward that the fae took, and was undeceived.

"We had some trouble," Althea said, her voice as light as his. "I take it you didn't know about the glass men?"

"Not a suspicion," said Carmine, his fingers running over Althea's damaged shoulder and then sliding down to her half-glass hand. "I would have stolen it myself if it wasn't for fae law. It's horribly restrictive in some ways. The human?"

"I healed his wounds," said Althea. "They were worse than mine. I almost lost him in the snow."

Carmine cocked an eyebrow at Markon and said to Althea: "Shall I fix this for you, sweetness?"

"Oh, why not?" Althea said tiredly. "Where's the girl?"

"The next room," Carmine told her. He inspected her hand first palm down and then palm up; and at last placed a long, lingering kiss in the centre of it. "That should do it, I think. It's the door on the right, if you absolutely *must* leave straight away."

Althea nodded and left the room with her hand curled once more in the folds of her dress, abandoning Markon to Carmine's curious gaze. Carmine looked at him for a very long time before he said: "Well done, human."

"You don't call Althea *human*," said Markon, rather tired of Faery in general and this fae in particular.

"Ah yes, but Althea is special," Carmine said. His heavy-lidded eyes surveyed Markon for some moments longer before he added: "I don't normally go in for this line of things, but I'm making an exception in this case. Treat her *very* well, human: and if I ever hear that you've given her one day's sadness I'll rip your innards through your throat and hang you with them."

"I think you've misunderstood the situation," said Markon.

Carmine gave him that crooked smile again. "Have I? I think not."

"Misunderstood what, exactly?" said Althea's voice. She was in the doorway with a thin young girl that Markon only just recognised as Parrin's first sweetheart, and she was looking distinctly suspicious.

"Nothing," said Carmine and Markon together.

That only made Althea look more suspicious, but all she said was: "We should go now, Markon. Lady Milee would like to get back to her parents as soon as possible."

"Tch, tch," chided Carmine. "Aren't you forgetting a little something? I believe you have a bauble of mine."

Althea said: "I don't think so."

"I distinctly recall it. I stood right here, and you stood right there. Handshakes, promises...does it begin to sound familiar to you, sweetness?"

"I said we'd steal it," said Althea. "I didn't say we'd give it to you."

"Now then, neither you did," said Carmine, with an odd smile that went all the way to his eyes. "Perhaps you're more fae than you thought."

"Perhaps," said Althea, and there was a touch of sadness to her eyes. "Goodbye, Carmine."

"Keep it for me, then. Until next time, sweetness. Until next time."

## 9

## DAY NINE

"What do we know– absolutely *know*?" asked Markon wearily. His back had troubled him all of yesterday and through the night with ice-cold pain that was only now slowly passing away, and he had not slept well.

"Our attacker is a woman," said Althea, offering him a mug of hot chocolate. It was already too warm in the library but Markon accepted it anyway, and Althea sat briskly down beside him, her back very straight and prim. "She's not a magic user, so she either bought the spell or someone gave it to her. Annerlee knew who she was, and the Doors have all been in the castle or the courtyards, so she has to be an inhabitant of the castle."

"What about the princess? She was attacked by bandits in her own lands."

"She was at the castle before that, though. All a fae would have needed is a cutting of hair or nails. They'd have followed that scent across the worlds if necessary."

"It's a pity Lady Milee couldn't tell us anything," Markon said; though he did wonder if it was a case of *couldn't* or *wouldn't*. The girl had been terrified, hysterical, and determined only in one thing: to be sent back to her parents in the grasslands of central Montalier.

Althea's little mouth grimaced slightly above the rim of her mug. "I'm not sure we could have trusted anything she told us: she's in a rather *delicate* state of mind. Some humans can't bear Faery."

Markon, his thoughts skipping ahead, said: "You said the other day that Doctor Romalier was moved after he was murdered. Is there any way to find out *where* he was murdered?"

"I asked Sal about that last night while you were sleeping," said Althea.

"Oh you did, did you?"

"I couldn't sleep," she said, and Markon saw the unconscious flexing of her left hand on the seat, the fingers that had been glass. "Besides, I met him while we were both prowling the halls and he said he'd answer my questions if I answered his."

Clever Sal! thought Markon, in some amusement. He'd straight away picked on the best way to deal with Althea.

"What did he say?"

"Amazingly little," Althea told him. "I've gotten more out of clams."

Markon couldn't help grinning. "Sal has a talent for saying very little. What did you do?"

"I repaid the compliment," said Althea, but her eyes were amused. "He did tell me that there were scraps of combed wool all over Doctor Romalier's body."

"He was wrapped in a sheepskin rug to be moved," said Markon, pleased to find that he understood. "All the guest rooms in the castle that are away from the furnaces have them on the floors."

Althea nodded. "Yes, that's what I found out as well. We had a lovely little walk around the guest quarters checking empty rooms and knocking on guest doors."

"Did you tell the guests what you were looking for?" asked

Markon apprehensively. He could only imagine how furiously offended the Count and Countess of Doute would be if told that his seneschal was looking for a murder scene in their rooms. Not to mention Pilburn of Wyndsor, who was also quartered in the guest wing and whose nostrils would undoubtedly quiver with outrage at the slightest breath of suspicion.

"No: Sal thought it would be best to tell them that some of the rugs had been contaminated with the sheep rot, and to take them with us."

"Did they believe you?"

"The Count and Countess did," said Althea. "They couldn't get rid of them fast enough. They had the full amount."

"Pilburn?"

"He had the full amount too, but I don't think he believed us. He wouldn't let us take them, at any rate."

"*Was* one of the rooms missing a rug?"

"The guest room across from Pilburn was missing one of its rugs," nodded Althea. "I thought that was very interesting, don't you?"

"Interesting but not very helpful," said Markon regretfully. "Was Pilburn aware that you were checking the other rooms?"

"He watched us from his doorway the whole time with his nose twitching," affirmed Althea. She chuckled suddenly. "Sal was very...*dour*...about it."

"Dour enough to offend?"

"Yes, but all under his breath."

"Well, I suppose we can rejoice in small mercies for that," said Markon.

"Pilburn did ask a lot of questions," Althea added ruminatively. "He was very intent upon knowing what I knew– what Sal knew, too, for that matter. Oh, he was also keen to know when he'd be able to meet with you: apparently he's asked to see you twice in the last few days and been turned aside each time."

"I'm living the day at the expense of the morrow," Markon

said, somewhat ruefully. "I don't particularly want to see him. He's been especially prickly since Doctor Romalier was murdered."

Althea looked rather thoughtful at that. "Perhaps he thinks he's next. That might explain why he's so interested in what *I'm* up to as well as what Sal's up to. Maybe I should frame him for the Doctor's murder just to keep him out of the way. He's by far too inclined to poke his nose where it isn't wanted. After all, it was Doctor Romalier who was supposed to be investigating the curse, not Pilburn."

"Honestly, if it wasn't for the fact that we know we're looking for a woman, I'd be tempted to think he did it. And if it wasn't for the fact that it must have been someone with a talent for magic who made the spell for our mystery woman, I'd think he did that, too."

Markon sank into the brocaded seatback and met Althea's amused eyes. "There's no real foundation for it, of course," he added. "Except that Wyndsor was *so determined* to send him here with Doctor Romalier. And if our records are accurate, he was also here as an envoy in the first Wyndsor/Montalier meet and greet half a year before the curse began."

"The meet and greet was to signal the start of real peace for you, wasn't it?"

"We hadn't had more than a few skirmishes for years before that, but it was the official treaty, yes."

"Well, if it comes to that, I don't see why someone else couldn't have given him the spell to carry with him. It's just a matter of how high you think it could go, and of how knowledgeable you hold Wyndsor to be."

"Pilburn could have sniffed out a malcontent while he was here first," said Markon slowly, beginning to sense a thread of real possibility in what had started out as an unreasoned suspicion. "His trunks were clear of magic when he arrived the first time, but a month or so after the team from Wyndsor arrived a few of them were taken on a tour of Montalier's inner cities. None of them were subjected to security measures when they got back."

"Our mystery woman, then," said Althea: "Do you think he found her by chance, or was he sent to find her?"

"If we're dealing in hypotheticals, I'd say that he found her by chance," Markon said. He discovered that he'd finished his mug of hot chocolate, and since that didn't seem to be an ideal state of affairs, he poured himself another. "We all but forced Wyndsor into the agreements: they were very bitter about it all. I don't particularly like my borders being routinely raided and it seemed expedient to do something about it."

"I read about the campaign," Althea said. Her eyes were distinctly amused. "I thought it was exceedingly clever."

"We were lucky that it rained when it did," said Markon carelessly, but her appreciative amusement was sweet to him. "Things could have gone harder with us if it hadn't."

"You went out with your men for the run, didn't you?"

"It didn't seem fair to ask them to risk making fools of themselves without doing the same," Markon said. Willing to change the subject, he added: "I don't think Wyndsor were so well prepared as to have a sleeper in my court, but I do think that they would have taken advantage of whatever unrest they could. If Parrin were to live and die childless, it would be much easier for them to subsume us: some Montalierans would even consider it better to be ruled by a foreign royalty than by a king who wasn't born to the throne."

Althea looked impatient. "How ridiculous! When it comes to the point, even your line wasn't always royalty, as ancient as it is."

"Treason!" said Markon, laughing. "Ah well, speculation bakes no pies, after all. We said we were going to talk about what we *did* know. Has there been any fae magic in your new suite?"

"No," said Althea. "But then, I've taken care to ward my room rather strongly now. I've still got the shard, by the bye. May I keep it?"

"I don't see why not," said Markon. "I doubt there's anything Montalier could do with it that Avernse won't do twice as well."

Althea, looking troubled, failed to acknowledge the compliment. "I'd like to know why Carmine gave it to us."

Markon looked at her curiously. "He didn't. You tricked him out of it and the girl."

"Yes, I think that's what he'd like us to believe."

Markon thought it over, and found that he agreed. He opened his mouth to ask what she thought Carmine meant by it, but found himself asking instead: "Did he really try to buy you?"

"A few times," said Althea, with a small smile that worried Markon slightly. "Not all the fae are the same, you see: they don't reason like us and I don't think any of them quite see us as equals, but they're not all monsters. At first I thought it was only kindness in him, trying to rescue me. Then I realised that he was actually interested in me."

"Wouldn't your mistress sell you?"

"Master. No. He was trying to drive the price up and he didn't like Carmine much. I think he enjoyed watching him get rebuffed."

"*Did* he get rebuffed?"

Althea's cheeks went slightly pink, and she sipped her hot chocolate with great attention. "I may have let him kiss me once or twice."

"*Really?*" said Markon with great affability. To his great amusement, this made Althea's colour deepen.

"Well, he was a very good kisser, and I was only eighteen! I knew exactly what kind of fae he was and the sort of fun he liked to have with fae or human women. I had no idea that it was marriage that he was after. If I had–" Althea stopped and considered this, frowning.

Markon, his amusement suddenly and utterly deserting him, said: "Would you have married him if you'd known?"

"Perhaps," said Althea. She looked up at Markon and the frown cleared away as suddenly as it had come. "I'm glad I didn't know. I made my own escape on my own terms. Carmine is rather delightful but he's also rather exhausting."

She curled her fingers around the dwindling mug of hot chocolate and fell into an appreciative silence, which Markon was happy enough not to break. He had his own thoughts to think, and if they weren't exactly pleasant, they weren't unpleasant either.

It was only after he'd disposed of his mug on the occasional table beside the armrest that a weight nudged itself into his shoulder, and he realised Althea's silence was because she'd fallen asleep. It seemed a pity to wake her, so Markon gently removed the chocolate mug from her fingers and placed it beside his own. Then he manoeuvred himself into a more comfortable position, put his feet up on the footstool, and went to sleep as well.

10

## DAY TEN

Markon woke with a feeling of deep satisfaction quite some time after midnight. He was confused to find himself sitting in the library, his back sore and his neck stiff, one weight across his stomach and another against his shoulder. Althea muttered in her sleep and shifted beside him, bringing Markon to the pleasant realisation that it was her arm curled around his waist and her cheek resting against his shoulder. Someone had also tossed a rug over them, which brought another memory with it: his steward entering the library to discover if he required anything. Markon, warm and comfortable, had said sleepily: "Just a blanket," and gone back to sleep. He grinned at the darkened library. Apparently his steward had done just as he was asked.

Althea muttered again and tried to shift her legs, but since she'd curled them up beneath her on the couch some time during the night, the action almost sent her tumbling from the couch. Markon caught her before she fell and said: "Careful, darling," without thinking.

"Ow," said Althea thickly. "Can't feel toes. Where am I?"

"The library," said Markon, propping her against the seatback before she could wake properly. "You fell asleep again."

"Oh," she said, half-heartedly swiping a hand across her face. Then, eyes snapping open, she said: "*Oh!* What time is it, Markon? Is it much past midnight?"

"A little," he said. The chimes had sounded for a quarter to four just a few moments ago. "Are we visiting Faery today?"

"Yes, I think so," Althea said, lifting the rug and looking around her doubtfully. "Where are my shoes, Markon?"

"Under the cushion," said Markon, unable to repress a grin. "Can you feel your toes now?"

To his delight, Althea sat down and wiggled them quite seriously. "Now I can. Was I talking in my sleep again?"

"You were. Do you often talk in your sleep?"

"Quite often," she said, slipping her feet back into her shoes. "Hopefully we can be in and out quickly today: I took a piece of magic from the hairless girl that I'm fairly certain is Seelie, so at least we won't run into any old friends this time."

"Well, that's something to be thankful for, at any rate," said Markon, happy to be spared another Carmine. After all, Althea was all but engaged to Parrin– an argument, he was well aware, that bore less weight in the light of his own behaviour toward her. He would have to be more careful.

Althea looked more amused than insulted. "Honestly, Carmine is about the sum of it when it comes to friends in Faery. It isn't a place that encourages friendliness."

Markon thought of the glass spikes that had all but ended his life and said: "It's not, is it?"

The Door let in a blinding light that almost felt warm. It was so bright that it took several minutes for Markon's eyes to adjust, and when they did there was still such a moving glitter of light on water that it was hard to tell what they were looking at. He hadn't expected to see water, and the instinctive step he took forward had Markon stepping into Faery just a little before Althea, who only just seized his hand in time.

"You're getting awfully casual about walking into Faery," she said, releasing him.

"It's beautiful!" Markon said. For the first time when entering Faery, it felt as though the sunlight was actually touching him. He found himself on a rock ledge that was being lapped at by the sparkling sea, a vista of sun, sea, and island stretching out before him. He walked on ahead of Althea eagerly, making his way over the rocky ledge until he could look straight down into the water, and found to his delight that he could see right to the bottom. It looked shallow enough to wade in. Behind him, Althea was frowning, her eyes darting from island to island and scanning the gentle waves. Markon wasn't sure if she was looking for something or if she recognised the place. If so, lucky Althea! He hadn't seen anything so alien or exotic in his life: the very air was heavy with heat, the waves turquoise and inviting. They looked cool, sparkling and clear– or *almost* clear. Was that something curving through the water?

Behind him, Althea said slowly: "Oh. Markon?"

"Mm?" There *was* something in the water. A flash of something pale, and ripples of golden...was that *hair*?

"Do you remember me saying that we shouldn't run into any old friends in Seelie cantons?"

A radiant face broke through the water, followed by a woman's shoulders and torso that were almost indecently free of clothing. She smiled at him, as beautiful and inviting as the waves.

Markon said: "Yes, I remember."

"I think we may have run into some old enemies instead. We'd better go back and try another piece of magic."

He thought he was safe. He wasn't close enough for the lady in the water to reach him, he was certain. The sandy bottom seemed so clear that he was assured that it couldn't be too deep.

And yet, when Markon turned to say: "I think you should see this, Althea," he only had time to feel something icily cold grip his ankle before he was hauled backwards with incredible strength into the sea. He heard Althea scream for the brief second before his ears were plunged below the water. Then he was swallowed by salt waves that curled around his arms and legs until he could barely move, the world a riot of sand and sea and sky.

Markon's first thought was, ridiculously, that the water was far, *far* deeper than it had appeared from his rock ledge. The clarity with which he could see the sandy bottom had deceived him, and no matter how often it flashed past in his spiralling descent, it didn't grow any closer, though it remained just as clear. His second thought was that the water was neither as restrictive nor as cold as he had at first thought: the reason he couldn't move his arms and legs was because the golden-haired fae had wound herself around them, and her skin was icily cold to the touch. Cold, smooth arms wrapped around his torso, stronger than seemed possible for so delicately formed a creature. Below that an eel-like tail encircled his legs, effortlessly crushing. After that it was hard to concentrate on any thought but his desperate need for air. As the last of it left his lungs and bubbled upwards in its eagerness to see the sky, Markon convulsed within the waterfae's embrace, salt water engulfing his nostrils and flooding his mouth.

There was an explosion of bubbles in a fierce arrowhead somewhere nearby. Markon, certain that he was to be drowned, found that the waterfae had put her mouth over his, breathing salt and fish and most importantly, *air*. Impossibly and unpleasantly, he was breathing again, though the water still closed around him suffocatingly.

"Better?" asked a bell-like voice. That was impossible, too, and Markon was fairly certain that he wasn't actually *hearing* it. There was too much salt water in his ears to hear anything. Cautiously, he nodded.

There was a tinkling laugh, like wind-chimes. "I forgot your kind can't talk here. Never mind, soon we'll be somewhere you can talk and eat without taking in the sea. I'm going to let your legs free now, pretty thing: we need to keep going. She'll catch us if we wait any longer, and that's a bit too soon for my liking."

She, who? wondered Markon. He could no longer tell what was up and what was down: the water was significantly darker where they were now. And then, as the waterfae loosed his legs and used that powerful tail to propel them, he saw Althea over her shoulder, dark in shadow with a face so pale as to be almost glowing. She was in her shift and swimming after them with powerful, practised strokes that seemed to be helped on by magic, so swiftly did she move through the water. Her eyes were fixed on Markon, and she didn't appear to have any problems breathing. *She*, Markon realised coldly, and fought to be free of the waterfae.

"Don't be nasty, pretty thing," said the fae, readjusting her terrifyingly strong grip. "I don't want to have to break your darling legs."

Markon was still struggling gamely when the waterfae darted around a formation of what he was reasonably certain was coral, and wrapped herself around him again. "Just you wait, pretty thing," she said, her hair settling around her head in an aureole. "Now the fun begins! No need to worry your pretty head about it: I'll make sure nothing hurts you."

There was a white blur in the darkness of the water and then Althea was there, still swimming determinedly after them. This time the fae let her get close, which worried Markon in a vague kind of way, and said: "You can't have him. He's mine."

"No he's not," said Althea, her voice odd and familiar all at once. It had something of the bell-like quality that the waterfae's had. "He belongs to himself. I suggest you let him go."

"You have such a lot of magic," said the waterfae, her eyes

calculating. "Clouding out like ink behind you and hiding things, but *I know who you are.*"

"What nonsense," said Althea, but there was a tension to her shoulders that Markon could see even underwater. "You're a silly little water sprite. What do you know?"

"I know about the changeling human who killed the king and stole his magic," said the waterfae. "And I know that the Queen wants to see you *so very much.*"

"Well, I don't particularly want to see her," Althea said. "Thanks all the same."

"I know," said the waterfae. "That's why I had to make you chase me. Oooh, she's going to be pleased with me!"

Althea's smile was a fearsome thing. "Only if you can catch me."

"I don't have to," the waterfae said.

To Markon, unfamiliar with his watery surroundings, it seemed as though a shadow grew around them. That wasn't likely, leading to his next thought, that they were encompassed by a vast school of fish. A few moments later it was obvious that it was neither shadow nor fish– in the strictest sense of the word. No, an army of waterfae had segued from the dark waters around them, myriad and multi-coloured tails undulating gently against the current, their silver armour palely gleaming in the small light that penetrated the depths.

"Let him go," Althea said. Her chin was set, as were her shoulders: she looked as though she was preparing to fight to the death. Perhaps she was. "If I have to fight my way out of this, a lot of you are going to be hurt."

"Yes, but if I see even the tiniest spark of magic from you, I'll break his pretty neck," said the waterfae who held Markon. Her slick fingers slid up and around his neck, twisting together until Markon's face felt tight and hot and ready to burst at the seams. He opened and closed his mouth, desperate to tell Althea to go, to leave him to the results of his own folly; but the constriction around his neck and the water in his mouth didn't permit him to do anything but gulp.

And Althea said simply: "I yield."

They were escorted with triumphant speed through the dark and oppressive waters until Markon began to see light softly disseminating through the current. At first, too disoriented to know up from down, he took it to be the sun, and hoped soon to break free of the water. As the light grew closer, however, he saw that it beamed from a domed source on what he soon recognised to be the rocky, sand-teased bottom of the sea. They approached it at great speed, Althea in her own little circle of waterfae and Markon still held hostage by the female waterfae. The dome increased in size so rapidly that it actually seemed to be growing. By the time they were near enough for Markon to see the vague suggestion of a city through the dome, the dome itself towered over them. When they were only a few feet away he could no longer see around it and the top seemed as far out of sight as the surface above.

"Here we go, pretty thing," said the waterfae, and pressed them both into the dome. Something cool and slightly resistant met Markon's face; then they were through, and there was actual *air*. Air, and freedom from the constant touch of water on his skin. Oddly enough, the sense of pressure only increased, bringing with it a heavy feeling of oppression. It didn't occur to Markon that the waterfae couldn't possibly move through this habitat with their long, supple tails until Althea was thrust through the dome after him, the fae who escorted her emerging face first, their tails shortening and separating until they stood on two legs. His own fae had done the same: and like the others, was now the possessor of a pair of muscular, finely-haired legs that were covered only to the knee by armour or—in his captor's case—a graceful fall of light fabric that dried immediately upon entering the dome. Althea's shift had not done so. She looked so small, defenceless and bedraggled that Markon could only wonder exactly what it was she'd done to be gripped so savagely on either side by two of the biggest fae he'd seen yet.

"Don't dawdle, pretty thing," said his captor. She forced Markon forward on a slick, shell-encrusted road that wound its piebald way through rows of equally shell-encrusted houses. Some of them were much the same as the houses back in Montalier, high and balconied and graceful, while others were more fanciful in design. Markon lost count after the first five conch-shaped houses, and didn't bother to try and number the houses that were formed in the shape of a sea-snail's shell: they appeared with a frequency that could only be ascribed to a current fad. And high above them, filtering a dark green light on the city below, the dome itself arched: untouchable, vast, and impossibly crushing.

The ground began to incline beneath their feet before very much longer. The houses were blurring around him, but it wasn't until the sea-shelled road also began to blur beneath his feet that Markon realised someone must be shortening the road ahead of them. He journeyed by magic quite often in Montalier and had never quite managed to get over his dislike for travelling under someone else's power, despite his Doctors' assurances of the safety of it. Here under the dome in Faery, it felt even more perilous.

There was a subtle sense of stomach-churning halt, and a doorway solidified ahead of the group: huge, double-doored and intricately carved.

*We've arrived*, thought Markon, his breath coming just a little too fast. *Whoever it is we came to see, we've arrived*. He looked for Althea between the muscled arms and scaled armour, but all he could see was the edge of one powder-white cheek and one glittering blue eye. Then the double-doors ahead of them were opened in a heavy sweep of stale air, and Markon lost sight of her in the forward torrent of waterfae that forced him into the foyer and up the cold marble stairs.

They were expected: the first set of double-doors on the landing was wide open, and when the guard of waterfae jostled Markon and Althea into the room, a woman in blood-red robes of lightly wafting silk was waiting elegantly on a dais at the end of the room. The guard stopped a respectful distance away, propelling both Markon and Althea to the forefront of the group, and waited at salute until the elegant woman nodded careless at them.

She had dark, brilliant eyes that pierced the room above a mouth painted exquisitely red, and when her eyes lighted upon Althea those scarlet lips curved in a thin, deadly smile. "My dear, it's wonderful to see you again," she said. Her voice wasn't loud, but it somehow carried throughout the entire room. "I have to admit, I wasn't expecting to see you! I *did* think that with the little accident that occurred when you left..."

She let the sentence trail off suggestively, and even Markon, who very much wanted to know how this tale fit together—had Althea *killed* a fae? Or was his understanding of the situation confused?—felt chilled.

Althea said quite calmly: "It wasn't an accident, Moriwen."

Those sharp black eyes narrowed, then a laugh rippled out. "You always were a truthful one, weren't you? Really, I should be rewarding you: thanks to you, my situation is very...pleasing. But I do think that regicide ought to be discouraged, after all; it really wouldn't do if my subjects felt they could dispose of me at a moment's notice and with no reprisals."

"That would be dreadful," agreed Althea.

"I didn't actually think I'd have to do it, you know. I thought you'd be too sensible to come back here again."

Althea shrugged one shoulder. "Yes, so did I. Accidents will happen."

"Oddly enough," pursued Moriwen; "I would have sworn that you'd fight to the death rather than be brought back here. Which brings me to the question of who *is* this delightful human? Never tell me he was used as leverage? My dear! How...*touching!*"

"Very human of me, wasn't it?" said Althea.

"The human side of you is *not* what worries me, my dear," said Moriwen. "It's unfortunate that you decided to return to my canton. I really rather admired what you did. However, it's no use mourning over what can't be changed. Your execution will take place tomorrow. Take them both to the Hold and make sure you put the human to sleep."

Execution! thought Markon, stunned by the rapidity of it all. And tomorrow! Around him the fae guard were murmuring their *Yes Majesty*s. In his ear, the female fae whispered: "Sorry, pretty thing! If you're lucky, they'll let me keep you. But the changeling human has a way of turning luck." She hauled him after the rest of the guard while Althea was pushed ahead, the white of her shift visible through the moving fae.

Moriwen's voice, amused, distant and cool, said as they left the room: "I know it's dull, my dear, but I won't feel quite comfortable until you're safely in the Hold. Even your significant magic will find it difficult to escape banded iron."

Iron made no sense, thought Markon, force-marched down flight after flight of corkscrewing stairs. The Hold was apparently far below the sea-shelled roads and cut deep into the rocky sea-bed: all reasonable enough for a waterfae. Iron, though? How could the Fae imprison *anyone* in iron if they couldn't even touch the stuff? But when they arrived at the bottom of the stairs, it was iron just the same. A dome reminiscent of the larger dome outside, the Hold was formed from band upon band of metal bolted together and overlapping each other, a great messy pile of menace to which none of the guards seemed to want to get too close.

One of the fae opened the curved door with a pair of manipulating sticks and a degree of skill that suggested he had done it many times before, and to Markon's outrage Althea was bodily tossed into it without regard to either her dignity or her limbs.

"She said to put the human to sleep," said one of the guards, his disinterested eyes lighting on Markon.

"I'll do it," said the female fae who still held Markon. "*Go to sleep*, pretty thing. Things will be nicer when you wake."

There was a frozen sliver of time between the moment Markon realised she'd laid a spell on him and the moment he realised that it hadn't worked. The fae's eyes narrowed as he remembered his iron bands in a shock of relief, and Markon slumped immediately, hot and cold with hope.

One of the fae chuckled. "Resistant little thing, isn't he? Oh well, he's gone now. Throw him in."

They were no gentler with Markon than they had been with Althea. It was nearly impossible not to try to break his fall; but it was over so quickly, the door slammed shut again with such dispatch, that any movement that might have betrayed him was lost in the shutting of the door.

Soft, cold hands cupped Markon's face before he could gather his shaken limbs together enough to rise or even open his eyes to check for damage. "Markon! Oh, Markon, I'm so sorry!"

"So am I," croaked Markon, discovering the discomfort of a cut lip and wondering if his eye was as swollen as it felt. He opened his eyes and found Althea staring down at him with her mouth open, a halo of glow bugs clinging to the iron above her head.

"You're awake! How are you awake? I heard her say the spell—I *saw* the magic go out!"

Markon grinned, pulling painfully at the cut on his lip. "Maybe I'm immune to fae magic."

She went for his wrists at once. "Why didn't you tell me you had dispelling bands?"

"I forgot I had them," said Markon, fending her off and

tugging at his wrist-laces until his cuffs were over the bands again. "I'm rather glad I did have them, aren't you?"

"Yes: for all the good they'll do you," she said. The glad light was already fading from her eyes, shadowed by the iron frame around them.

"I'm awake. We'll work it out from here."

"There's no working it out. I can't use magic to get us out of here because of the iron, and you can't open locked doors."

"We'll work something out," said Markon again. "We stole a Fae relic from a glass mountain and escaped being made glass ourselves. We can escape an iron–"

Althea's bitter laugh cut him off. "We can't, you know. This place is– well, I grew up here. It's not...it's not a nice place."

"Althea–"

"Not now, Markon," she said wearily. The soft light from the glow bugs seemed to smudge her face: she looked physically sick. Her back was still as straight as ever, but there was a terrible rigidity to it.

"*Now*," he said firmly. "Did you kill someone?"

"Yes."

"Did you kill their *king*?"

"Yes."

"How? *Why?*"

"He was my master. He was the one Carmine tried to buy me from. By then I was so crazy from the...the horrible pressure of here that I would have been glad for it. Glad to be bought and sold like a pair of shoes. I can't bear to be *squeezed* like this."

"This king you killed: was he the one that stole you?"

"Yes. They like to do their own work sometimes," said Althea, coiling his wrist laces around her fingers. "Do you know, he kept me on a leash until I was fifteen. He said that I needed to be broken to heel."

"He did *what?*"

"He'd take me with him when he left the dome and give me just a *little* bit of air. Then he'd let me off my leash."

"How much air?"

"Never enough to run away. Only enough so that it seemed possible."

There was a slow, cold rage coiling around his stomach. "Did he give you air in the same way that fae gave *me*–"

Instead of answering that, Althea said: "I knew there was a day coming when he'd either sell me to Carmine or give me an...*official* place in his retinue. It might have happened that way if I hadn't developed a talent for magic. He saw it and decided it was too dangerous to let me keep it."

Markon frowned. "To *let* you keep it? It was yours. How could he prevent that?"

"He tried to steal it. He often took me to other cantons—I was never sure if it was to bait me or them—and so it didn't seem odd when he took me across to one of the Unseelie cantons. Seelie don't do spells that steal magic or life, you see. They're above all that nastiness. But they will pay the Unseelie to do it for them."

"I see," said Markon, chaffing her hands. They were far too cold and his wrist laces had knotted around her fingers. "How did you manage to turn the tables on him?"

"You learn a lot about magic, living with the Seelie," said Althea. "Almost by accident, but more if you pay attention. The spell he put me in was a big sprawl of parts and chalk over a wooden floor, and I could tell enough of what it was to know what he was trying to do. I thought– I thought there was no hope for me, and I knew I'd live and die underwater with this horrible *pressure* always hovering over me. Then I saw that the only thing regulating the direction in which the spell worked was a little rod of wood. It was so tiny and light, and it turned without moving a hair of the rest of the spell."

Markon realised that he'd stopped chaffing her hands and began again.

"I was sure the Unseelie fae had seen me do it," Althea said. The straight line was between her brows again. "I was *sure* he had. But he went ahead with it anyway: started up the spell, then winked at me and left. When– when my master stopped screaming and withered into a ball in his section of the spell I thought I'd only stolen his magic. I didn't know—I *should* have known—that it would kill him."

"How could you possibly have known?" murmured Markon.

"Fae are all magic, especially their nobles," Althea said, matter-of-factly. "Snuff that, and they're gone altogether. It should have been obvious to me. I still wonder if I'd have done it if I'd realised."

"He would have done the same thing to you."

"Yes, but I wouldn't have died of it."

"No, you'd have died of old age in Faery, still under your master's control."

"Yes," said Althea. "I think that's why I couldn't be sorry. Not really. At the time I was just so sick and glad and horrified that all I could do was run."

"Where did you go?"

"Nowhere in particular. It was hard to get used to his magic, the way it moved and reacted, and I spent a lot of time just learning how to use it. So long as I kept moving I was safe enough, and after a while I began to hear rumours of a Door between here and there."

She was a little brighter, Markon thought. Perhaps a little more hopeful. It seemed good to foster distraction, so he said: "A Door like the ones in my castle?"

"Yes, except this one was open from the Faery side," said Althea, sitting up straighter. There was a touch of colour to her cheeks again. "There aren't a lot of them: they take immense power to open, and I wasn't sure enough of my new magic to try one myself."

Markon felt a dawning of cold realisation. "That espionage magic in your suite, the spell you said was made of fae magic–"

Althea looked slightly apologetic. "It really was fae magic. It's just that it was *my* fae magic. I didn't expect anyone to make a move against me in that way, you see. I felt a drain during the morning but I'd just been in the Infirmary and a slight drain is normal when I finish off a healing spell, so I didn't pay any attention. It was very cleverly done. Someone formed the espionage spell from my own magic, and then told Doctor Romalier what to expect."

Markon began to laugh. "And you simply told them the truth!"

"Yes," said Althea, catching a little of his mirth. "Honestly, I was half-afraid I wouldn't get away with it. It was a bit of a nasty moment."

They sat without speaking for a few moments, Markon's silence appreciative, Althea's thoughtful. Then she said: "I may have an idea of how we can get out of here."

"They won't come for us for a while yet," said Althea. "They'll unlock us tomorrow, but they'll send us a meal first. They like their ceremony, and it'll give them time to gather a crowd. The important thing is that they'll only send one fae with breakfast– or two at the most."

"That sounds reasonable," said Markon, beginning to understand. "They'll know I'm asleep, after all."

"And *I* can't use my magic in here," said Althea. "That'll put them off their guard enough to bring the meal right into the Hold. How are you at hand-to-hand fighting?"

"I make do," said Markon, who was still an enthusiastic and well-practised part of the Montalieran Weaponless Unit. Something about the quality of his smile as he said it must have satisfied her, because she nodded decisively.

"You'll have to be on the floor when they come in," she said. "Somewhere near the door, I think. They won't come in if they don't think you're under the influence of the spell."

"Wouldn't the iron from the cage stop the sleeping spell anyway?"

"No. If I'd put the dispelling bands on you after the fae put you to sleep it wouldn't stop the spell, either: the iron only prevents any new magic from sparking. They'll be convinced that you're asleep. Use that advantage, because it won't buy you much time once you get up."

"What then?"

"Up the stairs and out of the dome," said Althea. "They'll have the keys to get out. We'll only have half an hour, maybe less, and if they have to chase us they won't try to capture us again. They'll just kill us."

Markon hadn't expected anything else. He said, lightly: "That sounds fair. What now?"

"Now we wait until tomorrow."

"I thought they didn't have day and night here."

"They don't. Not exactly," Althea said. "They decided by consensus how long a day ought to be and then made it law. It may be the only law that both Unseelie and Seelie abide by. Unseelie put out their lanterns for night and Seelie like to sleep under the sun in their disgustingly picturesque bowers anyway, but neither of them need more than four or five hours of sleep. When they say tomorrow, it means after their sleep cycle. We've got quite a few hours to wait yet. You should try to sleep."

"Only if you do," said Markon.

He did intend to sleep. There were a few somewhat smelly but really very comfortable seal-skins in the iron cage, and it was surprisingly pleasant to stretch out below the glow-worms with his arm supporting Althea's head. Much to his relief, she went off to sleep straight away, and though it didn't quite take the tension from her face it did ease the crease in her forehead. Markon, settling himself to sleep, found that his mind was moving too fast and with too many thoughts to be able to relax.

Foremost of these thoughts, was the rapidly growing and

excessively inconvenient one that it was impossible that Althea should marry Parrin. If it was only the dismaying, delightful fact that he'd fallen in love with her, he would have made more of an effort to fight the feeling, but it had occurred to him at some stage in the last few days that perhaps Althea wasn't completely indifferent to him. For a moment or two it had even seemed as though she might– but what was the use of that? thought Markon wearily. There was the contract they'd signed. It seemed to hang before him when he closed his eyes, Althea's neat, precise writing spelling out the terms of their agreement, their signatures side by side. He'd looked at it often enough. Althea, in recompense for having broken the curse, was to be wed to–

Markon's eyes flicked open and he grinned joyously up at the glow-worms. There was no curse. There never had been a curse. It would be enough to break the contract, at any rate. And later there would be time to persuade Althea that marriage to him was, after all, more appealing than marriage to Parrin.

Markon closed his eyes and waited for the fae who would bring their meal, his lips curving in the darkness.

THERE WERE TWO OF THEM. Markon heard their footsteps on the stairs and quietly woke Althea, then took his position by the door. Althea stood straight and poised at the other side of the cage, her eyes glittering in the shadows, and Markon closed his eyes as the fae manipulated the door open once again.

He couldn't see them, but he felt draft of the first fae as it stepped over him.

"You might as well both come in," said Althea dryly. "I'm not likely to overpower you without my magic, now am I? Nor am I likely to eat all of this, so help yourselves."

Another draught swept overhead. Markon's eyes snapped open and he rolled silently to his feet behind the fae who had just entered, hoping with all his heart that fae had much the same physical weaknesses as humans.

He punched the first fae by his temple. The fae dropped to his knees with a surprised grunt that made the second fae turn, dropping the tray of food to draw his dagger. Markon kicked the first fae out of the way and stepped lightly forward to meet the second just as Althea smashed the tray over his head. If the tray had been heavier it might have worked: as it was, it merely seemed to anger the fae, who said through his teeth: "I'll deal with you next, changeling human!"

Markon sidestepped a lightning fast sweep of the dagger and closed with the fae quickly, gripping his wrist and twisting it as he spun away again. The fae broke free with a punch to Markon's stomach, but the dagger clattered to the rocky floor and was immediately pounced on by Althea. To Markon's relief she didn't try to interfere again: she stood by in perfectly composed silence as the fae faced up to him and said: "You'll live to regret that, human. Not for long, but you will."

"We don't have much time," said Markon, smiling grimly at him. "So if you wouldn't mind fighting instead of talking, I'd appreciate it."

He went in for the punch while he was still talking: a quick, twisting uppercut that would have landed beautifully if the fae hadn't also twisted at the last moment. It knocked him sideways despite that, and Markon closed again swiftly, following it with two quick punches to the fae's stomach. He didn't duck quite quickly enough, and took a hit to the temple that made his ears ring and his knees buckle slightly. The fae, sensing weakness, took two swift steps forward and was met by a double-fisted uppercut from Markon. This time it connected with a force that snapped the fae's head back and sent him straight to the ground with a sickening crack of head meeting rock.

"It's a good thing I hit him on the head first," said Althea into the silence. Her eyes were the lightest Markon had seen them since entering the waterfae's dome.

Markon burst out laughing and grabbed her hand. "I can't thank you enough! I couldn't have managed without you! Shall we leave?"

"As quickly as possible," said Althea, and threw the fae dagger down beside its owner.

They took the Hold keys and left the fae locked together in the cage. Markon was reasonably certain that at least the bigger fae was dead, but he didn't want to take any chances; and as Althea said, any time bought for them while the fae unlocked the door to the cage was time gained.

At the top of the rocky stairs they had to wait while a laughing, merry group of fae swept down the street, their eyes bright.

"They're going to the execution," said Althea in Markon's ear. "They're already pretty high and happy, so it won't be long before the other guards come after us. The Queen likes to make sure the crowd's at fever pitch before she starts an execution."

"How civilised," said Markon, and cautiously cracked the door open again. Althea slipped through first and he followed close behind, trusting to her sense of direction when it came to the dome. Behind them the noisy group of fae danced its way up the streets and merged with another, larger group that was also sweeping through the houses.

"This way," said Althea, and hurried down a narrow walkway that opened into the next street. When they stepped into the street he thought it was familiar, but it wasn't until Markon followed the direction of Althea's eyes that he recognised where they were.

They had come back to the house in which they'd met the Queen.

"Wait here," said Althea. She was pale but determined. "There's something I have to get first."

"Althea–"

"I know," she said, and ran for the great double-doors. Markon followed her at a carefully casual walk, his eyes darting up and down the street, but it was empty. Even the faint sound of the distant mob of fae ceased when he stepped into the foyer and hurried up the stairs after Althea. She met him at the top of the stairs in a flutter of white cotton, something small and metallic clasped in her left hand, and dragged him back down the stairs.

"Back the way we came!" she gasped, leaping the last few steps to the first floor.

They tumbled out onto the street at a run, Althea leading the way, and when it blurred around them Markon was for once not at all uneasy about travelling under speed of magic. He'd heard the ominous babble of fae voices rising again, and even as they moved along the streets at impossible speed, the back of his neck crawled with the awareness of the fae weaponry behind them. Then there were shouts and the drumming of feet, and he was too busy running to have any attention to spare for the shivery feeling that tried to tell him he was about to die very quickly.

They hit the edge of the dome before Markon was ready for it, plunging into the icy, pressing embrace of the sea while he was still gasping for breath. Salt water flooded his nose, but Althea was already forcing air into his mouth just as the fae had done earlier, albeit more pleasantly and with less of a fishy aftertaste. While he was still coughing on the seawater that had seeped in through his nose, she gripped him under the arms and bore him upward through the tugging current in a swift and disorienting spiral. Markon wasn't sure if it was his imagination or if there really was a spreading cloud of waterfae polluting the water below them, just too far out of sight to be discernible as such.

He was sick with relief when he saw the ripple of light playing across the surface above them, and when they burst from the surf and into blessed, dizzyingly light freedom he hauled Althea from the waves without taking a moment to enjoy the delight of it. She was shivering in the warm air but Markon didn't mention it because he had discovered that he was shaking too, and that it had nothing to do with the temperature.

Althea's dress was still on the sand, a puddled mass of blue brocade that scattered sand and several tiny crabs when she picked it up and shook it out. Markon expected her to pull it back on but she hung it over her arm instead and said through her shivers: "We'd better get back through the Door before they find us again."

"You can't walk around the castle in your shift," he protested, ridiculously shocked.

"Rather that than be caught again," said Althea, with perfect good sense, and led the way back into the human world. She struggled rather damply into her dress again once they were back in the castle. Fortunately, despite what a dismayed Markon realised to be the noon sunlight outside, the hallway wasn't busy in the slightest, and she was able to do so unmolested.

Watching her pull her laces tight one-handed, Markon said: "That'd be easier if you passed me the shard."

Althea laughed and tossed it to him: blunt, broken and not particularly shiny. She wasn't shaking now that she was back in the human world, and Markon was glad to find that he wasn't, either.

"Is it part of the same sword as the other piece? And how did you know it was there?"

"I saw it when we were dragged in front of the Queen," said Althea. "Even if I hadn't seen it, I would have *felt* it. I'd rather give both shards to Carmine than let something like that stay with her."

"Your next puzzle," Markon said lightly; and when Althea was finished dressing he gave it back to her.

His guards, excellent fellows that they were, didn't so much as turn their heads when Markon strolled past them, trailing sand and dripping seawater, and vanished into his suite. Parrin must have given orders, however: Markon was in the process of stripping his wet clothes and towelling himself dry when his son entered his suite at a decidedly quick walk.

"I told Sal you'd be back before nightfall," he said. Despite the lightness of his voice there was a touch of relief to his smile.

Markon left his changing to hug Parrin briefly and roughly. "I couldn't leave word. I'm sorry."

"It's all right. Sal told me you were with Althea, so I knew you'd come back safely. I hope you don't mind: I told everyone that you were sick and took all your audiences today."

"Good lad!" said Markon, smiling at him. Parrin had been trained to run the court by himself, but he'd never been thrown into it without notice before.

Parrin flushed slightly and tried not to look too pleased. "You've got bruises on your stomach," he said. "And one next to your eye. What were you up to?"

"That," said Markon, sighing with relief to be dry again; "Is a very long story. You'd better sit down."

## DAY ELEVEN

Why was it, thought Markon in irritation, that whenever he wanted to talk to Althea, she was nowhere in sight? He'd slept later than he meant to, but he'd still been up and awake in time to allay the concerns of both his steward and Parrin, who seemed to be of the opinion that Markon was as feeble as a new-born calf.

"Thank you!" Markon had said acerbically, resisting Parrin's solicitous attempts to help him into a dressing gown and shrugging a light jerkin over his shirt instead. "Parrin, I realise I won't see forty again, but it's really not necessary to treat me like a senile old man."

"Not senile," said Parrin soothingly. "Just a bit tottery!"

"Where's Althea?"

"You couldn't expect her to be here while you're getting dressed!"

"I didn't expect you to be here while I'm getting dressed, if it comes to that!" retorted Markon.

"Why *are* you here? It's not that I don't love you, but I'd rather not be bundled into my dressing gown and slippers."

"Althea said you might still be weary. She said to let you

sleep."

"That's very kind of her," Markon had said, and he'd gone in search of Althea despite Parrin's protests. The amount of information that they'd gained from Faery was seeming increasingly less worth the risk of entering it, and he thought that he'd like to catch her before she gathered any more magic and made her plans for the forthcoming night.

Unfortunately for his plans, the day was a busy one. Even after the midweek hearings were done with, small, petty problems sprouted from every conceivable task, stretching out the time he was obliged to spend on them; and when in frustration he at last sent for Althea, not even his steward could find her.

And that, thought Markon as he went down to dinner, was exactly like her! She was probably using a look-away type spell to wander the halls unmolested. His annoyance was only compounded by the fact that every person he met seemed to find it necessary to ask about his health, and after dinner he stole away to his library to get some peace and quiet. There was more work to do in the library, of course, but it was possible to ignore the paper-strewn desk if he wandered through shelves of books instead. The windows were a nice distraction, too. They looked out over the gardens, which at night were festooned with tiny pinpricks of light that managed to illuminate an improbably large area of greenery. Markon, smiling indulgently at the few pairs of lovers who were making use of the softly-lit walks, caught sight of a familiar couple and felt his stomach drop.

Althea and Parrin were in the garden, talking. Just like the day he'd interrupted them in the library, they were sitting very close together on the garden bench and leaning intimately toward each other.

*I was wrong*, thought Markon, as Althea put her hand on Parrin's shoulder and smiled at him. *I was very, **very** wrong*. There was a leaden weight around his neck that seemed to be slowly choking him as he turned blindly from the window. The contract...well, at least the contract wouldn't need to be broken. Markon sat down at his desk, tidying a pile of papers and gathering his pens back into their holder. The ink bottle was missing, and that suddenly seemed important enough to merit a complete clean of his desk in order to find it. Slowly and methodically, Markon began to clean his desk.

The clock system had already signalled the half past eleven when Althea burst into the library, her blue eyes glittering. Markon looked up from his spotlessly clean desk, wishing that his heart wouldn't leap so betrayingly every time she appeared.

He said: "You've been busy, I take it?"

"I know who did it!" Althea said. "Come along, Markon, I have to show you something!"

"Where are we going?" demanded Markon, but she'd already darted from the library again, her feet quick and light. He gave chase but Althea flew down the corridor ahead of him, just out of reach, her laugh floating back to mock him.

There was a Door down the stairs and around the corner, though Markon's guard was nowhere in sight. More worrying than that was the fact that Althea had obviously left the Door open while she came to fetch him. Had his man gone through?

Althea smiled at him from the cusp of the Door and stepped through without waiting for him to join her. Markon, unwilling either to be left behind or let her go by herself into Faery, stepped from the corridor and into a typically Seelie forest, the sun filtering through the trees above with a gentle glow. It looked familiar. Markon threw an uneasy look over his shoulder at the door and saw with that it had closed completely, the forest an unmarred expanse of green and gold behind him. He drew in a long breath through his teeth: let it out slowly through his nose.

"You're not Althea, are you?"

Althea rippled slightly in the soft air of Faery, and was quite suddenly no longer Althea. Markon took in the aged face with its golden eyes and cruel mouth, and recognised the first fae he and

Althea had encountered in Faery. "You'd best come along to the cottage, human," she said. "I'd rather not cross your lady, myself, but I'm Burdened to do so."

"I'm not going anywhere with you," said Markon. He had his iron bands; and more importantly, proof positive that they worked. He was rather weary of being told what to do by the Fae.

The fae made a sharp motion at him—a spell of some kind, Markon thought, with a faint smile—and her eyes grew as hard as chipped amber when it became evident it wasn't working.

"Got you under protection, has she? Well, come or stay as you will. You'll not get back to the human world now."

In the end, Markon went with her. She couldn't harm him with magic, and it was unlikely that such an elderly fae could do him physical harm so long as he didn't let her get behind him with a weight in her hand again. Besides, he had a feeling that someone awaited them in her cottage, and since it was most likely to be the woman who had summoned the fae, Markon thought it expedient to find out who she was.

The elderly fae didn't speak to him as they walked, she merely muttered to herself and wheezed a little. Markon helped her over a shallow stream at one point, somewhat ironically amused to find himself helping the fae who had been sent to kidnap him, and though the fae didn't thank him she did stop her muttering. She also stopped glaring at him every time he walked a little too quickly for her, and when they reached the cottage she stopped him at the door with one claw-like hand.

"Not much I can do to you now," she said, and Markon was surprised to hear so little bitterness in her voice. Now she only sounded tired. "That glamour I worked on you was almost the last of my power. But that girl– she's the kind that'll dig out your heart with a spoon if she's not got a knife. Don't show her your back, human."

There was a hooded figure by the fire-place when the fae showed Markon into her sitting room. As far as he could tell with her hood drawn, she seemed to be gazing into the ashes. One hand was propped against the mantelpiece, causing her cuff to fall back from her wrist where a plaited bracelet of faded red thread clung. A memory turned, whirred, and clicked in Markon's mind: Parrin as a little boy, sick and bundled up so much he could scarcely move, plaiting bracelets with an upper maid.

"Nan!" he said. "It's Nan, isn't it?"

She turned to face him, shrugging off her hood. He remembered her from the upper kitchen as well, where she'd looked resentfully at Althea and made remarks about the kind of opportunistic women who tried to break Parrin's curse. Today she merely looked satisfied.

"Now you remember me," she said. "Of *course*. Now that I've been forced to bring you here."

"I'll put the tea on," said the fae, rolling her eyes. Markon felt a strong desire to laugh. She'd evidently had bear Nan company for some time now.

"You're the one who's been opening Doors to Faery," he said.

"I shouldn't have had to," said Nan, with a look of cold dislike. "We were promised to each other, Parrin and I. But there's always someone trying to take what belongs to me, so I did something about it."

"Why did you send someone to get me? I'm no use to you."

"I don't care about *you*. But she'd go through all the cantons of Seelie and Unseelie just to find you, and I want *her* very much. She knows who I am."

"Who are you talking about? Who is it you want to trap?"

"Me," said Althea from the door. "It's me you're talking about, isn't it, Nan?"

Nan's face gained some animation in triumph. "I knew it! I recognised you because I'm just the same, and I knew you'd come."

"Well, here I am. What do you want with me?"

"Kill her," Nan said to the fae woman. "She knows it's me."

"So do I," Markon said, as the elderly fae drew herself together wearily for a fight he was certain both she and Althea knew she couldn't win. "Are you going to kill me, too?"

The girl's eyes focused on him, and she said: "Yes, you'll have to kill him too."

"If she tries to harm either myself or Markon, it will kill her," said Althea warningly. "Look at her! She's got so little magic left that she can't even regenerate it. She's dying."

"I don't care," Nan said sulkily. "The fairy godmother gave me the spell, and she *has to obey me*."

Althea sighed. "All right, then. *Fae, I bind you!*"

The fae woman, white as chalk, stopped in her tracks with fear written across every line of her face.

"Good," said Althea. "Now sit down and for pity's sake drink some of that tea before you collapse! I'll deal with you later."

The fae said: "Ooof!" and sat down thankfully. "Don't mind if I do."

Markon passed her a cup and saucer because it seemed only polite, and poured out for her with the same faint feeling of hilarity that he'd had before.

"You're a good human," she said to him.

"*Don't* feed the fae," said Nan. "She's meant to be doing her job. Why is everyone always against me?"

Althea, who had been watching Markon pour out with some amusement, said: "I can't think why. I left you a little something at the door, fae. Markon, we should go now."

Markon looked up just in time to catch the flat, poisonous look that Nan directed at Althea.

"I won't go with you," she said sullenly.

"You'll have to," Althea told her. "That poor fae is at the end of her magic: there's not a thing she could do to stop us going back to the human world and taking you with us, even if I *hadn't* bound her."

"And there's the little matter of facing trial for murder, conspiracy, and treason," said Markon grimly.

"Well, I won't," Nan said again, but when Althea prodded her forward in the small of her back, the girl trotted along ahead of them resentfully. Markon wasn't entirely sure that she had any idea of the kind of trouble she was in: she seemed content to mutter of their perfidy as she was slowly but surely edged back outside the cottage.

"We'll all go through together," Althea said, when they were in sight of the Door again. No, not *the* Door. *A* Door. It wasn't the one by which Markon and the fae entered Faery. "This Door opens in Nan's room, and I don't want her darting away either here *or* there."

"I won't run away," said Nan. "I didn't do anything wrong. People are always trying to take away the things that are mine, and it's not fair."

"Did Annerlee try to take away what was yours?"

"She was talking to you. She shouldn't have done that."

"She didn't tell us anything," Althea told her, propping the Door open. "She was too afraid of you. You didn't have to kill her."

"I'll take her arm," said Markon, sick to his stomach at the girl's utter indifference. He reached for Althea's hand with his spare one.

"All right," said Althea, as Markon stepped through the Door. "But we'll have to watch out for–"

Markon arrived in Nan's room while Althea was still speaking, and found that he wasn't alone. There was something boxlike sitting on Nan's bed, and at the foot of the bed was Pilburn. As Althea segued from Faery with Nan, Pilburn said: "Please don't move. The spell is poised to start at the *least* quiver of my finger, and I assure you that the fae it summons has more power in her little finger than is in the entirety of this puny kingdom."

## 12

## DAY TWELVE

"That's what I was trying to tell you," said Althea regretfully, while Nan scuttled away behind Pilburn. She closed the door to Faery with a casual sweep of one hand and added: "He's the one who gave Nan the summoning spell, aren't you, Pilburn?"

"Amongst other things," said Pilburn, with a sharp, toothy smile. "You should take better care of your subjects, your majesty. Dissatisfaction in the court can get very messy, can't it?"

"So can spells," said Althea. "I *really* wouldn't start up that spell if I were you, Pilburn."

Nan said disgustedly: "Don't listen to her, she's just trying to frighten you."

"It's unfortunate," Pilburn said. "I didn't want to kill you, your majesty. Not yet, anyway. But at least Parrin is poised to take the throne, even if the poor boy will never be married."

"Why kill the Doctor?" asked Markon. It was clear that Pilburn was on the point of starting up the spell, and it was possibly best for all concerned that he didn't manage to do so. "You're both on the same side."

Pilburn gave a short, impatient shrug. "That man! He actually thought he could stop the curse! I had to come along to make sure that he didn't interfere with Nan; which was unfortunate, since it put me back in a position to be discovered."

"He came into your room that night without knocking, didn't he?" Althea said. "He was pompous like that, sailing in and out of apartments without notice. I'd say he walked in to find you and Nan with the spell in front of you."

"Close enough," said Pilburn. "He would have recognised what it was immediately. The fool thought we were really trying for peace with Montalier! He thought he was helping! At least he was easy to kill: I called him over to look at the spell and slit his throat before he even saw the dagger."

Nan, fidgeting with her fingers, said: "He shouldn't have bled all over the rug. There was blood underneath and it wouldn't all scrub away."

"You took the sheepskin rug from the opposite room to cover up the stains," nodded Markon.

"Did you carry the Doctor to his room by yourself?"

"He was too heavy," said Nan. "Pilburn helped me and then he went away with the rug. He should have stayed and slit *her*, too." There was that flat, venomous look again, thought Markon, chilled.

"Nan was arranging Doctor Romalier's body when Parrin and I walked in," said Althea, unaffected. "It was a clever idea to pretend to faint: it hid the blood on your apron. It was only this morning when I thought about it that I realised you were a recurring thread in the tapestry. You were there when the doctor was murdered. You were Annerlee's closest friend—did you know she was holding the quilt you tatted together when she died?—and when I asked Parrin last night about the upper maid who played with him when he was sick, he remembered you very well."

"He was supposed to be *mine*," said Nan. "You don't understand. We loved each other. We would have been married but the king arranged for an advantageous marriage instead. What was that to our love?"

"Parrin chose his own bride," Markon told her gently. She looked at him without recognition, and he wondered if she remembered he was the king. "There was no arrangement, just love."

"Liar," she said. "I know he loved me. We were promised to each other."

"All those girls, Nan! The ones that died, or were injured, or stolen!"

"It's no use talking to her," said Pilburn, with a rude laugh. "She's as bent as a cornerstone."

"So that's why you were in Annerlee's room," said Markon. "You thought she'd hidden the spell there and you were afraid she was getting too unstable."

"I did the right thing," Nan said serenely. "I know, because my fairy godmother gave me the spell, and she wouldn't have done it if I wasn't in the right."

Pilburn muttered in disgust: *"Fairy godmother!* You addled little wench, *I* gave you the spell!"

There was a malevolent gleam to Nan's usually dull eyes. "You're a liar, too," she said. "Open, open, *open!* You're summoned!"

They seemed like nonsense words until Markon realised that a Door to Faery was once again opening right there in Nan's room. His stomach dropped in dismay and he looked instinctively down at Althea, who smiled calmly at him and threaded her fingers through his. She wasn't afraid. But why–? No, *who?*

The door opened fully, and when the fae stepped through Markon recognised the Lady of the Revels. "Here I am again!" she sighed. "Heigh-ho! Did I not warn you of the consequences of summoning me again, humans?"

"You'll do as you're told," said Pilburn. "You're Summoned and Burdened. You'll take your instructions from me."

"No she won't," Nan said, with an angry light in her eyes. "She'll take them from me!"

Althea said: "I don't think she'll take them from anyone, actually."

"What have we here?" said the Lady of the Revels. She was looking at the spell intently, her eyes avaricious and cruel. "Little one, did you do this?"

"Yes," said Althea. "They're all yours. If you want them."

"Oh yes, I think so!" the lady said, her voice coldly amused. "You, *come here.* You: *pick up the spell and come with me.*"

Pilburn, who had been watching them bemusedly, picked up the spell with stiff hands and marched toward her on legs that were just as stiff, his face draining of colour. Nan was there before him, her face very red and puffy, her eyes dark with anger.

"You can't have me!" she squealed. "My fairy godmother–"

"Be silent," said the Lady of the Revels; and Nan, her eyes bulging, was silent.

Althea said: "It's no use taking the spell. I've already ruined it and it wouldn't work from your side, anyway."

The Lady sighed. "I feared as much. Heigh-ho, one must take the day with its successes, after all! Farewell, little one: I appreciate your troubles. Humans: with me!"

She opened the Door again and vanished through it, dragging Pilburn and Nan behind her. The last Markon saw of Faery before Althea shut the Door behind them was Pilburn's despairing face and Nan's furious one, lit by the silver light of the Unseelie moon.

"That's that, then," she said, with the smallest huff of a sigh.

"You *sabotaged* their spell," Markon said, grasping for understanding. "You knew it wasn't going to work the whole time."

"Exactly."

"But I was trying to distract him from starting it up!"

"It was very clever of you," said Althea apologetically. "And you did a wonderful job, but I must admit the whole affair stretched out a lot longer than I was hoping for."

"*When* did you sabotage it?"

"When I finally realised that it had to be Nan," Althea told him. She looked rather annoyed. "I could kick myself, Markon! Imagine being taken in by a pretend faint! By the time it fell into place for me and I'd thought to ask Parrin about Nan, she'd already gone into Faery. She left the spell here in her room, and it seemed obvious that if we got back either she or her benefactor would try to use the spell again to deal with us. So I tweaked it a little bit to make things fairer and came right after you."

"And Pilburn? How did you know it was him?"

"It wasn't very exciting," Althea said. "I went back to his suite late yesterday because it seemed ridiculously unhelpful of him not to give up his rugs to Sal and I, considering he likes to be thought of as helpful. One of the rugs had quite a bit of watered down and dried out blood beneath it. I don't think Nan knows much about scrubbing."

Markon found himself smiling. "Possibly not. Nor does Pilburn, if it comes to that."

"Will you wake Parrin to tell him the good news?"

"Oh, let the lad sleep," said Markon. He felt suddenly tired and very, very old. "I'd best start on the interminable paperwork if I want to find a tactful way to let Wyndsor know that we found the spy they planted in our court, and that he was the one who murdered Doctor Romalier."

"Shall I come with you?" asked Althea. She was looking rather thoughtful, and her blue eyes rested on him with a questioning air he didn't understand. "I think it may be time we discussed our contract."

"No!" said Markon, more harshly than he'd meant to. More carefully, he said: "You should get some sleep, too. Bring Parrin to the library at ten o'clock this morning and we'll discuss anything you want to discuss."

THE MORNING SPED by in a series of bells from the internal clock system until Markon, who was still doggedly working on an official report for Wyndsor's edification, realised that it had just sounded ten bells.

With the last bell the library door opened and Althea entered in a decisive kind of way, trailing Parrin behind her. She was too pale again, with deep purple crescents beneath her eyes. That, coupled with the fact that she was still wearing the same unassuming frock she had been wearing earlier in the morning, told Markon that she hadn't been to bed at all. What had kept her awake? It occurred to him that his brusqueness earlier in the day might have led her to think that he wasn't going to honour the contract, and a searing sense of remorse burned through him. Was that what she'd spent the morning fretting about?

Willing to atone for his mistakes, he said with a smile: "Ah, the affianced couple! Shall we make the announcement tonight, or are there to be special arrangements for a celebration?"

"Ah," said Althea, exchanging a look with Parrin. "So *that's*– I don't think you quite understand."

Parrin, meeting her gaze with what seemed to Markon to be distinct horror, said: "Good grief, no! I'm not marrying Althea!"

"There was a promise made," said Markon sharply. "You won't refuse to honour your obligations!"

"Actually," said Althea, her eyes light and bright; "You might want to look over the contract again. You can go, Parrin. I don't think we'll need you after all."

Parrin left swiftly: too swiftly, in fact, for Markon to either call him back or dismiss him as well.

While Markon was still staring perplexedly after his son, Althea wandered away to the window and gazed out at the view with her back very straight. Without looking at him, she repeated: "You might want to look over the contract again, Markon."

He looked at her back with narrow eyes and strode over to his desk. The contract was at the top of the first drawer where he would catch a sight of Althea's neat handwriting every time he opened it: one of those things that he'd not consciously done and now regretted.

"Read the last section," Althea said.

"I've already read it," said Markon, but he read it again nevertheless. *"'In the event that the aforementioned Althea of Avernse shall break the aforementioned curse and succour His Royal Highness Parrin of Montalier, she shall be recompensed as follows: at a time of her own choosing, to be made Queen of Montalier by marriage to the–"* Markon stopped abruptly, his mind spinning.

Althea said: "Keep going."

"*'–by marriage to the king.'* But this is nonsense: Parrin *is* to be king. You are to be queen."

"That's not what the contract says," said Althea, to the window. "It says *at a time of my own choosing*. I choose now."

Markon, his breath coming a little faster than he was used to, said: "Why me?"

"In Avernse there's word of a coming trouble," Althea said, still to the window. "Something so vast that it would reach even to the corners of the wild lands. Avernse and Montalier have always been good friends and the Queen thought it would be helpful to have one of us here when the trouble comes. She suggested that Parrin and I might do well together. Then I met you and you were rather nice, and I've never much cared for boys so I decided I'd rather marry you."

Markon felt a dull pain at the back of his throat. He said flatly: "You decided that you'd...*rather*...marry me?"

"I didn't expect you to be so lovely," said Althea, and Markon thought he saw the smallest trace of a smile in the reflection she cast in the window. "I thought we'd suit very well. And then I thought that maybe you were a little bit fond of me and that was nice and a little bit odd."

"Fond," repeated Markon slowly. "You thought I was *fond* of you."

"Well, I hoped so," said Althea's voice, through the pounding in his ears. "I got rather fond of you, you see, and that made it harder to tell. I did draw some redundancies into the contract, just in case you'd rather not marry me. The– the contract– well, it mentions *the curse*, and since there never was a curse as such–"

"You thought I was *fond* of you?"

Althea, her shoulders very stiff, said: "The Queen will be happy enough just to keep an Avernseian in your court. You needn't feel that you have to marry me if you'd rather not."

"I would rather," said Markon, slightly incoherently. "I would *very much rather* marry you."

That made Althea turn around at last, a flush of pink in her cheeks. "Are you sure? You don't have to feel obliged–"

"I don't feel obliged," Markon said, moving closer. There was a ridiculous gladness surging through him.

"And you shouldn't feel that you *have* to–"

He took another step forward. "I don't."

"Are you–"

"I'm sure," said Markon, taking advantage of the fact that he was now close enough to embrace Althea by wrapping his arms around her. He kissed her once, soft and glad, delighting in the way that her arms immediately curled around his neck, and said: "I'm very sure."

The second kiss was longer and decidedly more forceful, broken only to allow Markon seat them both on the couch and murmur: "In fact, I've never been surer of anything in my life."

And since he didn't like Althea to feel uncertain it seemed expedient to take the next few minutes to continue showing her exactly how sure he was.

Printed in April 2023
by Rotomail Italia S.p.A., Vignate (MI) - Italy